The Garnet Bro...

Katherine Goody

All rights reserved, including the right of reproduction in whole or in part in any form.

This book is sold subject to the condition that it shall not, by way of trade or otherwise, be lent, resold, hired out or otherwise circulated without the prior consent of the publisher in any form of binding or cover other than that which it is published and without a similar condition including this condition being imposed on the subsequent purchaser.

This novel is entirely a work of fiction. The names, characters and incidents portrayed in it are the work of the author's imagination.

Published in the UK by

Katherine Goody 2023

ISBN:9798854989756

DEDICATION

To Roger

With love and thanks for all your help and advice and for showing an interest in my writing, for editing this book endless times and for your patience.
You are such an encouragement; I couldn't do it without you.
Thank you too for the artwork and design for the cover.

I love you.

Acknowledgements:

St Mary & Ethelburga Parish Church, Lyminge Archeological Project, Lyminge Historical Society and Pathways to the Past, for providing the historical background that has inspired The Garnet Brooch. Mike Parry for the graphics and Debby and Matthew Jones for all your help.

Year 2019 Main Characters

Hilda Hogden aka Granny Hogden

Erin Hogden - Granddaughter

Max Judd - Archaeologist

Derek Trott - Archaeologist

Jo & Hetty - Publicans of the Coach and Horses

Professor Crump - Lecturer at Canterbury University

Cherry Smithers - Assistant Lecturer

Charlie - Old school friend of Erin's

Great Uncle George - Granny Hogden's brother in law.

Bill & Pat - Jo's friend and partner

Year 634 Main Characters

Elfin - Young Saxon girl

Alfric - Messenger to Queen Ethelburh

Ilfred - Elfin's Father

Borwood - Ilfred's friend
Bryce - Borwood's son

Rowena - Elfin's sister

Queen Ethelburh - Queen and Abbess

PROLOGUE

In 633 Queen Ethelburh, or Ethelburga as she is often known in modern times, fled from Northumbria to the safety of Limin (now known as Lyminge.) Here she founded a double minster or convent for men and women, becoming the first Abbess.
When she died in 647, she was regarded as a saint and her remains were placed in the northern porticus of her church as she requested.

****

Ethelburh reined in her dapple grey mare and raised her hand to signal to her entourage that she wished to stop. She looked out over the green and verdant countryside that lay before her. Softly rolling hills and woodland, with streams flowing down to the valleys where sheep and cattle grazed. So peaceful, so beautiful. Her beloved Kent, how good it was to be home, away from the fighting and her unsettled life in Northumbria. When her husband King Edwin died at the Battle of Hatfield Chase, she knew it was time to leave. Life was becoming increasingly difficult for her and she was constantly afraid that her life was in danger.
Ethelburh, was the daughter of King Ethelbert and Queen Bertha of Kent, who through St. Augustine's influence brought Christianity to the Kingdom of Kent. After Ethelburh married Edwin, King of Northumbria, she lived there for many years amongst

the turmoil and fighting. Her brother King Eadbald was now King and she was looking forward to seeing him again.

Turning to her handmaiden, Ardith, she smiled. 'Our new home, we are safe at last.'

'How far is it my lady to the settlement of Limin, will we get there before the sun sets?' asked Ardith.

'Now we have passed Cantwareburh, it will only be a few more miles. Eadbald said he would meet us there. My heart grows warm within me as I think of our reunion. It has been a long time.'

The route from Cantwareburh to Limin was a straight one and they covered the distance with ease, arriving just as the last rays of sun disappeared behind the clouds. King Eadbald was waiting for them outside the royal property at the centre of the village. The royal residence was his gift to her, a place which had royal heritage, probably built by the Romans before their return to Rome. A place that was fit for a Queen.

Eadbald ran to help Ethelburh from her horse. 'My dear sister, wilcume it is so good to see you and know that you are safe. Come I have prepared a feast in your honour, let us eat, drink and be merry.'

Ethelburh shook off her travel robe and Ardith put a gold cloak around her shoulder, fastening it with a brooch. It was delicately crafted in gold, intricately woven and with small red garnets around the edge. In the centre was a large garnet encased in a star. As she entered the residency, she held her head high, every inch a queen, the brooch glittering and sparkling in the flaming torches that lit her way.

The Garnet Brooch

CHAPTER 1

2019

'What the…' said Erin as she leaned heavily on her horn. 'That was a bit too close for comfort.' She'd forgotten how the M20 was a rat run for lorries going to Dover and the Channel tunnel. Most of them were foreign drivers who didn't care which side of the carriageway they drove on and seemed to take great delight in pulling out without any form of indication 'Idiots the lot of them', she said, turning up the radio. It was Steve Wright in the afternoon, one of her favourite programmes; she used to be a radio one lover but now preferred radio two. 'I must be getting old!' she laughed to herself. It had been a while since Erin had visited Kent and memories came flooding back as she continued her journey to Lyminge. Memories of her teenage years before she'd gone to St. Thomas' to train as a nurse. Wild nights at the Cameo in Ashford, dancing the night away to the sounds of The Black Eyed Peas, Lady Gaga and Beyonce. She used to stay with her friend Ruby who lived in Ashford. They would have great fun getting dressed up for a night on the town, in very little at all. Granny would have had a fit if she'd seen her. It would be so good to see Ruby again, she must try to get in touch. The last she had heard was that she had four children and was living in New Romney with an artist. Ruby was always a bit of a wild child. Erin came off the motorway at Ashford and took the country route towards Lyminge. She hated motorway driving and began to relax as she drove through the countryside. She knew the country lanes like the back of her hand together with all the pubs, The Woolpack at Smeeth, The Tiger at Stowting, The Dukes Head at Sellindge and the Drum at Stanford. She had such happy memories of The Tiger, all those crazy nights listening to blues and folk bands and drinking the night away. Then singing all the way home in her little Fiat. Those were the days. Taking the road to Postling, she continued on until she came to New Barn Corner with the golf club up ahead. Grandad had loved his golf and she had spent many a sunny afternoon as his caddy, but she never really understood why anyone would want to spend the day hitting small balls down a little hole. Granny used to say she thought it was a good walk spoiled. Turning left on Canterbury Road she smiled to herself as she passed Broadstreet House remembering the happy times she had spent caring for the residents there. People with learning difficulties always seemed so content with the simple things in life despite their problems. It didn't take much to put a smile on their face. It was there that she had felt the calling to train as a nurse. Then before her was the village sign, 'LYMINGE'. It had been fixed now, thank goodness. Last time she had visited some silly so and so had scratched off the LY. Not a very nice greeting as you entered the village. Driving into the village she felt she was journeying back in time to a place of peace and quiet where all was well with the world. It reminded her of the film Brigadoon. With Gene Kelly and Cyd Cherise, one of Granny's favourite films.

In a matter of minutes, she was at her destination, 'Lavender Cottage'. As she opened the door the cottage felt cold and empty, all was quiet except for the old clock ticking on the mantelpiece. Erin stared around the room, she could still smell the scent of lavender which Granny loved and feel her presence all around. Her favourite chair covered in a warm pink throw and fluffy cushions looked as though she had just popped out for a minute. She couldn't believe she'd gone, slipped away peacefully in her sleep. Granny was one of those constants in life, always there with a hug, cup of tea, and piece of seed cake. It was the end of an era, all her little knick-knacks and photos bringing back memories of different events in her life. So many photos, of family and friends. In a silver frame there was one of Granny and Grandad on their wedding day back in 1948, Granny looked beautiful in a white lace gown, which had been handed down through the generations and Grandad stood tall and proud in his Army uniform. Next to it lay Granny's brooch. It was round and looked to be about seven centimetres in size and made of gold. The body was a delicate filigree design, studded with small red stones around the edge and one larger stone in the centre of a star. It was edged with a gold rope design. Granny always wore it, she said it had been handed down through the family and it kept her in touch with the past. Erin was her only surviving relative and was in line to inherit the cottage with all its fixtures and fittings, plus a few small items including Granny's jewellery. She looked down at the brooch in her hand and wished she had paid more attention to Granny's stories; they may have told her more about her past and her ancestors.

Granny, aka Hilda Hogden, had lived in Lyminge all her ninety-eight years. She was born at Shilston House in North Lyminge and moved to Lavender Cottage when she married Alf. They had one son, David, Erin's father, who had been taken from her far too soon. Her great love of history, especially that of Lyminge, gave her an affinity with the past and she often held seances at the cottage, swearing she spoke to family from the Saxon times. You would see her on many an afternoon, sitting quietly on a bench in the churchyard of St. Mary & Ethelburga, amongst the dearly departed. Eyes closed and lost in her thoughts.

Erin had been born in Norwich and had enjoyed an idyllic childhood, until, at the age of seven, both her parents had been killed in a road accident. They had been driving home from the theatre when a deer ran across the road. Swerving to miss it, they drove head on into an oncoming lorry and were both killed outright. Following the tragic event, she went to live with Granny and Grandad Hogden in Lavender Cottage. Erin couldn't remember much about her mother and father except the fact that she always felt loved. Her father was a tall handsome man with a big smile and an even bigger hug. You always felt safe in his arms. How she missed him. She guessed that was why as a teenager she looked for love and affection in others, especially men. Even today she was still looking for that love and affection but sadly she always seemed to look in the wrong place and pick all the wrong men. She was currently between men. Richard, her last boyfriend, had gotten over possessive. He wanted to know where she was, who she was with and what she was doing every minute of the day. Even on her nights out with the girls he'd turn up out of the blue. His attention had been flattering at first but after a while she just wanted some time to herself. It came to a head when he started complaining about the long hours she worked at the hospital and told her it was either him or the job.

Lavender Cottage was a listed building, built at the end of the nineteenth century. A tiny little cottage with pink roses round the door, a low sloping roof and small leaded light windows. It had two small bedrooms upstairs and a lounge and kitchen downstairs. The small kitchen and bathroom were out the back, together with a sweet cottage garden. Located just across the road to the village pub, the Coach and Horses, and just a stone's throw from St. Mary and Ethelburga's Church. Erin had got used to the bells now, but they used to wake her up, ringing on the hour from dawn until dusk and on high days and holidays. Leaving school, she went to train as a nurse at St. Thomas' Hospital and moved to London. She had worked there for eight years now and didn't have much time for a social life as the work kept her busy. What she was going to do now, she wasn't sure. She had taken six weeks unpaid leave to sort things out with Granny's funeral and the cottage, but she couldn't think beyond that yet. Erin unloaded the car and took her bags up to the tiny bedroom that had once been hers. The stairs were steep and narrow, and the beams made the ceilings very low and she found it a struggle to get her case upstairs. She had forgotten how small the cottage was. Having unpacked, she decided to go over to the pub for something to eat.

The Coach and Horses was an old coaching inn built towards the end of the nineteenth century and could tell many a tale of the village and its residents. It had seen many changes over the years but the one thing that never changed was its warm welcome.
'Good evening, Miss Erin', said Jo the publican. 'Good to have you home. Such a shame about Mrs. Hogden, she'd had a good life ain't she, and passing away in her sleep, now that's the way to go. Ninety-eight, weren't she?'
'Yes, she would have been ninety-eight next week. It's funny here without her, I will miss her,' answered Erin. 'Has anything new happened since I left Jo, or just the usual peace and quiet as always?'
'Pretty much, except for the excavations up at the churchyard. They've got the University lot from Reading up there at the moment looking for more relics from the Anglo-Saxon settlement and the church. Think they've found a few things, which has caused a lot of excitement around the village. Folk are helping with the dig, brushing and washing things they find, it's all people are talking about. A walkway has been built at the church over the site of the old church and you can watch as they dig away underneath. You'll have to go and look.'
'I'll do that, I know Granny loved it up there and spent many hours sitting in the churchyard. I've the funeral

to sort first, I need to get a date booked and advise her solicitor before I do anything else. I do hope you'll be able to do the wake for us Jo? There won't be many, just myself and a few of her friends from the village, about a dozen I would think.'

'Of course, my lovely, it'll be my pleasure, you just tell me when. We'll give the old girl a good send off, and don't you go worrying, it's on the house.'

After a few glasses of wine and Jo's famous steak and ale pie, Erin was ready for her bed. She was very thankful she didn't have far to walk home.

CHAPTER 2

Erin had a peaceful night's sleep, she guessed she must have been more tired than she thought. It felt very strange being back in her old bed again and so quiet after living in London. Lyminge was a busy village with always something going on somewhere. It had two churches, a primary school and a smattering of shops, as well as the Coach and Horses and the Coffee Cabin. There was also an active bowls club, a cricket club and two doctors' surgeries. The pace of life was slow and peaceful, very unlike London with its endless traffic, high rise buildings and people of every nationality coming and going day and night.

After visiting the funeral directors, she decided to walk up to the church to have a look at the dig. They certainly were doing an impressive job. Looking down from the raised walkway she could see footings and what looked like the shape of an old church, beside today's church. Erin was deep in thought when she felt someone standing next to her.

'Hi there, I'm Max Judd, the director of the dig, haven't seen you up here before.'

'No, I've been in London working. I used to live in Lavender Cottage with my Granny but sadly she passed away last week. I've come back to sort things out.'

'Sorry to hear that,' replied Max. 'So, you'll know all about Lyminge and its rich Anglo-Saxon history then?'

'No, I don't actually, I moved away to London to train as a nurse eight years ago and never really took an interest in that sort of thing.'

'Well let me give you a bit of a tour then and fill you in with the history of this place.'

'That would be great,' smiled Erin. 'Thank you.'

'Where to start, well… As we look down, we see the footings of a seventh century church, which would have been part of the Anglo-Saxon monastic community. A mixed community of monks and nuns placed under the rule of the Royal Abbess, Queen Ethelburga. She was very influential in bringing Christianity to Kent and it's believed that this is where Christianity first gained a foothold in Anglo-Saxon England. Our excavations also show that Lyminge was an important royal site before the foundation of the monastery, and that its origins as an Anglo-Saxon 'Central Place' date back to the fifth century. Today's church was built originally as a monastery and housed both monks and nuns who were under the rule of the Royal Abbess Queen Ethelburga.

Queen Ethelburga died in 647 and was buried as she wished in the north aisle of the church in an unmarked tomb. This was exposed in 1860 by the Reverend Canon Jenkins during his excavations of the site and he recorded it with a plaque that you can see today, set in the side of the current church.'

He paused. 'Shall we walk down into the church, then you can see for yourself and we can look at some of the treasures we've unearthed?'

As they walked down to the church, Max noticed

Granny Hogden's brooch which Erin had pinned on her jacket. It looked very old and rather like some of the pieces they had unearthed around the dig. But no, it couldn't be, probably just a nice piece of costume jewellery.

They entered the Church by the South door through a wooden porch way that went over the ruins of the old Church. Erin stopped just inside the door, struck by its beauty. To her left was the bell tower and the church organ with its pipes reaching up high in the rafters. To the right ran an aisle flanked on either side by arched windows and oak pews leading down to the chancel and the altar. Above this was the most magnificent stained-glass window depicting Jesus and the prophets. The sun was shining, making a kaleidoscope of colours on the tiles below. Max led her to the north aisle where they were sorting through all the finds from the dig. There were items of jewellery, coins, pieces of pottery and old tools all providing clues as to how life was in Saxon times. 'You're doing an amazing job,' Erin congratulated the team as she and Max joined them.

'Why not come and join us, it's great fun?' said Angela, one of the village team.

'I just might do that,' replied Erin, ' I've a funeral to attend first, but then I'd love to.'

After looking at all the artefacts and drinking numerous cups of coffee, Erin said her goodbyes. As she left Max followed her outside. 'Lovely meeting you today,' he said.

'You too, thanks for the guided tour.'

'I couldn't help notice your brooch', said Max. 'Have you had it long?'

'It was my Granny's; she always wore it. It has been handed down through the generations, so I guess it must be mine now as I'm the last one in our family.'

'Mind if I have a closer look? It looks rather like some of the pieces we've found during the dig.'

Erin took it off and handed it to Max. He turned it over in his hands, licked his fingers and gave it a rub.

'Looks as though it could be gold and if so, those red stones are most likely garnets. Have you had it valued?'

'No Granny's always worn it, she said it reminded her of where she came from.'

'Well it could be very valuable if it's what I think it is. I should get it valued if I were you. I could take it to the Kent Archaeological Society (KAS for short) for you. They'd know. We take all our finds from the dig there for authentication. It's based at the University in Canterbury.'

'If you think it's worthwhile that would be great,' Erin replied.

'I am going tomorrow morning, you could come with me if you like. I'm leaving at about half-past ten.'

'I'll be ready and waiting outside Lavender Cottage, opposite the Coach and Horses. See you then.'

Erin was waiting on the doorstep as Max pulled up in his land rover. Leaving the village, they drove up Longage Hill and past Sibton Park cricket ground to Rhodes Minnis. A sleepy hamlet of pretty cottages and country lanes. Taking a left turn at the Lord Whisky tea rooms they continued on through the forest to Stone Street. At certain times of the year, Erin told Max, you might get a glimpse of a deer under the shadow of the trees. Stone Street was built by the

Romans and like many others of its time, it was as straight as a die, giving a direct route from Hythe to Canterbury.

At the service station they turned right on to Stone Street and headed towards Canterbury. It was a beautiful late summer morning and driving along they passed tractors in the fields gathering the harvest in. It had been a good summer and the bounty was plentiful. Birds swooped around the tractors as they went about their business and high in the sky you could see the skylarks dancing as they sang their merry song. Erin and Max chatted companionably as they drove the ten miles to Canterbury. Max told her what he had found out about the brooch on the archaeological website.

'Definitely looks Saxon,' he said. 'If it's made of gold, as it would seem, then it probably belonged to someone from the royal household. Brooches were popular in the sixth and seventh centuries,' he went on, ' worn by men and women, mainly to hold their cloaks in place, usually made of copper or silver. Only those of wealth would have a gold one, like royalty or rich landowners.'

'Do you really think it could be Saxon? I know it was passed down through the family, but I didn't think it was that old.'

'You never know,' Max smiled, 'you could even be a Saxon princess.'

'I wish I'd listened to Granny's stories. She used to say the brooch connected her with the past and she loved to sit in the churchyard at Lyminge surrounded by her ancestors. So you could be right.'

Arriving in Canterbury they went straight to KAS and

met Professor Crump, head lecturer and expert in arts and humanities. A short stocky man with large black bushy eyebrows. They made up for his lack of hair. The few strands he had were neatly arranged on top and pulled across in what is commonly known as a comb over. He wore a tweed jacket, green bow tie with a hanky in the jacket pocket to match. Baggy corduroy trousers and brown brogue shoes. In his hand he held a pipe which he didn't actually smoke but every so often he put it into his mouth to chew. He specialised in archaeology and he was a great favourite with his students due to his eccentric ways and enthusiasm. Having worked with the team from Reading on the dig at Lyminge, he was very excited to see Erin's brooch saying that in his opinion it was gold, pure gold, set with garnets and was nearly 1700 years old. The value could be anywhere between eighteen and twenty thousand pounds, depending on the authenticity of its provenance.

'A piece like this,' he said, 'should be in our museum of Saxon artefacts.'

'No, I am sorry that can't be, it's a family heirloom and as such it must stay in the family,' Erin told him.

'Can you prove that?' said the Professor. 'If you have only just found it , then it rightfully belongs to the state and the money is shared half and half. It would then be put on display in the museum for everyone to enjoy.'

'It belonged to Granny Hogden or I should say, Hilda Hogden and it's always been in the family. Now that she has passed away it has come to me as her only surviving relative.'

'It has to be proved,' said Professor Crump. 'Do you

have any evidence, a will or anything?'
'I am not sure whether Granny made a will, her solicitor is handling everything, I'll have to make enquiries.'
'Well I suggest you do,' replied the professor. 'This looks like a very significant find and as such should be in the museum.'
Max was looking on feeling rather guilty as poor Erin seemed very upset. He had hoped to help her not give her problems. It did look rather valuable, just imagine how much a gold brooch from the Saxon times could be worth.
They left the university in a sombre mood and made their way back to Lyminge.
'This brooch has always been in my family. It rightfully belongs to me, and I'll prove it,' said Erin.
'I am sure Granny will have mentioned it in her will somewhere, all will be well,' Max replied encouragingly.

The history of the Hogden family went back centuries and there was a strong connection to Lyminge and St. Mary & Ethelburga's Church. Perhaps there would be information in the church archives, she must try and talk to Reverend Good about it. If Granny hadn't made a will, how was she going to prove that the brooch was hers, oh why had she listened to Max and taken the brooch to Canterbury? If only she'd just kept it to herself, no one would be the wiser and she didn't really care how much it was worth. It was its sentimental value that was important to her.

CHAPTER 3

The next day was Granny Hogden's funeral. Predictably, the weather decided to take a turn for the worse and bang on midday, when the funeral procession reached the church, the heavens opened. The church was full, Granny had a great deal more friends than Erin had thought, and they had all come to pay their respects. Reverend Good gave a lovely service, sharing stories from Granny's life, together with other friends from the village. Erin spoke about the family, such as it was. She was the sole surviving relative, apart from a cousin Jonathan Daley, from her father's only sister. He read a poem. Then it was time to go out to the churchyard for the committal. The good Lord must have been smiling on Granny as the rain had stopped and the sun was starting to peep out from behind the clouds.

'Ashes to ashes, dust to dust,' Reverend Good prayed, 'we commit our dear friend Hilda Hogden into the merciful hands of God.'

He gave Erin a handful of earth and she threw it on top of the coffin alongside several flowers from other mourners. Reverend. Good continued, 'We will now say the Lord's prayer. 'Our Father who art in Heaven ....'

As they were praying Erin's thoughts went to Granny's

brooch which she had pinned to her jacket. Was it her imagination or was it speaking to her?

'Find the truth and set me free, my story will reveal the key. Hold the brooch within your heart, never let it depart from you. It is rightfully yours and not for the taking, after the setting of the sun, a new dawn is breaking.'

Suddenly Erin was brought back from her thoughts as a man next to her said, 'Amen,' very loudly in her ear. She took a deep breath and blew her nose.
'What just happened?' she asked herself as she followed the mourners back down the path towards the Coach and Horses.
There was no time to think. As she entered the pub, she was surrounded by well-wishers all giving her their condolences and telling her how wonderful Granny was. She was hugged and kissed by nearly the whole village it would seem.
'I do hope we have catered for enough', she said to herself as she looked across to the bar. Jo was there smiling away and as he saw her, he gave her a big thumbs up.
'Good old Jo,' what would she have done without him?
Turning, she saw Mr. Barnes, Granny's solicitor, tucking into a mouthful of prawn vol- au-vent and headed over to speak to him.
'Mr Barnes, thank you for coming, it's lovely to see how much Granny meant to so many people.'
'Yes, certainly a good turnout, Miss Hogden, and what a lovely spread the pub has put on for her.'
'When shall I come and see you regarding the reading

of the will?' Erin asked him.

'No need, I've just got a few loose ends to tie up and then I'll release the power of attorney to you as her only relative.'

'But what about the will?' asked Erin

'Oh, she never made a will,' said Mr. Barnes, 'so everything is straightforward and just goes to the next of kin, which of course is you. She had very little in the bank, no other investments, just the house and her few personal possessions.'

Erin was very quiet and felt rather faint.

'Are you feeling unwell?' asked Mr Barnes, quickly moving her to a nearby seat.

'Did she make any mention of this brooch?' She asked, pointing to her jacket. 'It was Granny's and could be very valuable.'

'No, no mention of anything that I've found so far.'

'Did she have any letters or documents, proof of ownership or anything like that?'

'Not that I've come across, but I'll certainly run a check for you. Don't worry my dear, things will sort themselves out.'

With that he made his goodbyes, knocked back the last of his wine, grabbed his coat and brolly and took his leave, with a promise of being in touch over the next few days.

The party was thinning out now as people made their way home. In the public bar Erin could hear the crowd from the dig laughing and joking as they talked over the finds of the day. Max appeared at the bar.

'Why not come and join us for a drink when you're done, we're just finalising the day's findings. Couldn't do too much with all the rain but we found a few interesting coins, which might prove valuable.'

After the last of the mourners had gone, Erin wandered into the public bar and headed over to where Max was deep in discussion with a group from the dig.

'There you are, perfect timing,' he said, 'I was just telling the guys here about your brooch.'

All eyes looked at the brooch on Erin's jacket.

'Oh, wow it's amazing, looks like a royal gem to me,' said a tall chap called Derek who was very intense and enthusiastic about everything Saxon. 'I'd love to have found something like that, it must be very valuable,' he continued. 'Could be one of Queen Ethelburga's, or one of her household, being gold and all.'

'I don't know about all that,' replied Erin. 'All I know is that it belonged to my Granny and now it's come to me.'

'Of course it did, of course it did,' he said, giving her a knowing wink as he walked away.

'Why does everyone think I've just found it? It's the truth that it was handed down through Granny's family. I am not making it up,' Erin said feeling very tired and emotional all of a sudden.

'Any luck with the will?' Max asked, 'Or proof of ownership?'

'Not yet but I'm hoping her solicitor will turn something up. It's Granny's, she was never without it. Possession is nine-tenths of the law, so they say.'

'Yes, but you are going to need some written proof, I hope you find it.'

'Well I am not going to find out anything this evening, so I'll love you and leave you. Thanks for the drink, see you soon.'

Leaving the pub Erin decided to take a walk up to the church before she settled down for the evening. Her thoughts returned to Max. He was a nice man, not bad looking in a rugged sort of way, very thoughtful and helpful. He had kind eyes, very blue and sincere and his tousled black hair curled over his collar, making her feel like she wanted to run your fingers through it. It wasn't the time or the place, but given the opportunity, he was a definite maybe. She smiled to herself as she walked up to the churchyard. What was she thinking, he was probably married? The sun was just setting behind the West tower and it shed a warm glow over the church and the dig. Erin sat down on a bench and took a deep breath in to calm her emotions and then sat with Granny's brooch in her hand wondering what secrets it could tell. Sitting there staring at the brooch it seemed to get warm in her hand and the world around her became still.

All was silent, a mist had formed over the churchyard and it floated gently on the breeze. She could make out a small figure in the distance, by her dress it looked like a nun, singing softly as she bent over the soil. Everything around her had changed, the churchyard was no longer there, the ground was ploughed and troughed and planted with an abundance of vegetables. She could see the old Church in all its glory, with another building where the war memorial had stood. The new church building looked like a monastery that obviously housed the nuns. From inside the church you could hear mass being sung, the gentle ringing of bells and the smell of incense filled

The Garnet Brooch

the air. Behind the monastery the land fell away, looking out over green meadows and copses of trees, with a stream that ran through the valley winding its way around hill and dale. Further ahead, she could see tents and simple wooden houses with domed thatched roofs, surrounding a more substantial building which looked like the residence of an important person. People were coming and going about their daily lives, cooking, gathering firewood and collecting water from the well. Dogs ran freely chasing the chickens and children played in the stream. Beyond it all was rolling countryside, no houses, no pub, no school, just green as far as the eye could see, dotted with sheep.

No one noticed her sitting there under the old tree, she was invisible to them. Erin sat in silence watching this new and fascinating world around her, it was though she had stepped back in time. All of a sudden, there was a shout and a loud bell rang out.

'Make way, make way,' came the call, 'for our lady Queen Ethelburh.' The bell rang out again and from inside the church appeared a tall handsome woman dressed in fine wool clothes with a golden cloak across her shoulders. She had beautiful curly auburn hair and walked with an air of authority. Passing close by to where she sat, Erin was able to get a closer look and there on her cloak was Granny Hogden's brooch. Erin couldn't believe it, it really was Granny's brooch. So it had belonged to royalty, Max was right but how did Granny get it? The Queen walked down to the settlement and entered the large building which must have been the royal residence and was gone.

'How can I find out more about the brooch?' Erin wondered. 'Did Granny just find it? But no, she said it had been in her family for generations. Someone must know.'

Max had been closing up the church for the night, securing down the dig and locking away their tools when he looked up and noticed Erin sitting on a bench in the churchyard. 'A pretty little thing,' thought Max. 'Rather intense though.' It was a difficult time for her, what with the family bereavement and everything. She seemed vulnerable and it made him feel protective, he wanted to wrap her in his arms and make everything ok.
His feelings surprised him. As he walked up to where she was sitting, he put his hand on her shoulder and found himself looking into a pair of deep green eyes. She stared up at him looking rather startled and disorientated and he wondered what was going on in her mind.
'You must have fallen asleep and it's getting dark, shall I walk you home?' he asked.
Bringing herself back to the present Erin pinned the brooch back on her jacket and followed Max back to Lavender Cottage.

CHAPTER 4

The year 633

Dawn was slowly breaking, the sky turning red as the sun rose over the settlement at Limin. Birds began to go about their daily routine raising their song in joyful anticipation. Elfin opened her eyes and looked around the home she shared with her father and sister Rowena. The fire was still smoking, and someone had put a pot on for their porridge. It was like most in the settlement, a one roomed building made from wooden planks, with a steep sloping roof made of straw. They had curtained an area off so the sisters could have a bit of privacy. Father slept on his mat by the fire. She rolled over on the straw mattress she shared with Rowena and put her hand to her belly. It had been six weeks now since her last bleed and she was wondering if she was with child. She felt worried, nervous and a little excited, what would Alfric think? They hadn't spoken of marriage, but she presumed he would ask for her hand after all they had been to each other. He loved her, didn't he? She would tell him tonight. Putting on her long woollen dress over her linen shift, she fastened it at the shoulders with two copper brooches, then tied it round the middle by a cord sash. After combing her fingers through her long blonde hair, she wrapped her woollen shawl around her shoulders. The day was bright, but a late summer chill hung in the air. The days were shortening, and it wouldn't be long before the winter solstice. Elfin was three years younger than Rowena and was prettier by far, turning the heads of many a man in the village.

Elfin and Alfric had met one day when she was washing clothes at the stream. He rode up on his black stallion looking very striking with his golden curls and red beard. He stopped to let his horse drink and as he dismounted, she noticed the red cloak he wore over his leggings and tunic depicting his status as Royal Messenger. He was of about average height, but by his build he gave the impression of being a warrior. They had talked together until the sun had set and it was getting dark. It was obvious from the first moment they met that there was a special attraction between them, their eyes held each other speaking of hidden promises, not wanting the moment to end. Elfin would go down to the stream each evening in hopes that she would see him again and he would be there standing under the great oak tree with his horse. Their passion for each other was like a drug and one kiss led to another, until they sought the darkness of the forest to release their desire. Her days were filled with cooking, cleaning and looking after the family home but her mind was never far from her handsome stranger, she couldn't wait for evening so she could go to the stream and find him. He told her his name was Alfric Huckbone, messenger to Queen Ethelburh, taking letters and important documents across the country. He had travelled with her from Northumbria and stayed as part of her household. When he could, he always tried to get back to Limin by evening.

Elfin waited and waited that evening but he didn't come, and she waited the next evening, and the next, and the next. Why hadn't he come? She was beside herself with worry. What was she going to do?

After two weeks when she arrived at their meeting place, a very tall man was waiting for her. He was dressed completely in green and was holding a parcel, wrapped in sackcloth.

'Godne aefen, are you Mistress Elfin of Limin?' he asked in a very deep brown voice.

'Yes Sire, do you have news for me of Alfric Huckbone?'

'He gave me this for you Mistress and asked for you to keep it safe until his return. He has to return to his family in Apuldre. His father is on his deathbed and they need him to take over the pig farm and provide for the family. He declares his love for you and wants you for his wife. If you are willing, he will return in the spring and claim you as his bride. I am to wait for your answer.'

There were tears in Elfin's eyes as she took the parcel.

'Thank you, kind Sir, please tell Alfric, I will wait for him, for ever and a day and that I would be honoured to be his wife. My heart overflows with love and I cannot wait to see him again.'

Her hand rested on her small rounded belly that was hidden in the folds of her smock. The news that he was to be a father she kept to herself, it was her secret and for now, she must keep it that way. The messenger took his leave and Elfin sat down by the stream to open the parcel. She unwound the sackcloth and there inside she found a finely woven shawl with embroidered lettering. An A and an E entwined in two hearts. It was beautiful and fit for a bride. Pinned to the shawl was a gold brooch with shining red stones around the edge and a large stone in the centre. It looked very valuable. 'I must find a safe hiding place for this,' she thought as she quickly wrapped it back in the sackcloth.

It was dark by the time she got home, Rowena was already in bed and her father was sitting round the campfire with their neighbours enjoying a glass or two of mead. She waved as she went inside and looked round for a place to hide her parcel. She could put it in the straw mattress, but Rowena was likely to find it there, or put it behind the log store, under the matting or high in the rafters above her bed. This was the best place she decided and found some twine to tie it safely to one of the beams. Tucked in the corner out of view of prying eyes.

It was October and the shadows were lengthening and the days becoming shorter. A time of mists and fruitfulness as the earth prepared for its winter sleep and all creatures great and small built their nests. Her morning sickness had passed now, she had managed to hide it from Rowena and Father, but it wouldn't be long before it was a secret no longer. Hopefully she would be able to hide it until the spring when Alfric would return.

CHAPTER 5

2019

Erin rolled over and as she stretched, she realised she was not alone. Max was sleeping soundly beside her, a look of peace and contentment on his face. 'Looking under the covers she realised she was completely naked.
'Oh goodness, what have I done?' she said to herself.
She quickly jumped out of bed and went in search of her dressing gown, then went down to the kitchen to make herself a strong cup of coffee. Sitting coffee in hand she went over the events of the night before.

They'd walked back from the churchyard in complete silence. When they reached her front door Max asked gently, 'Do you want to talk about it?'
She wasn't sure she knew what had happened, she hadn't got her head round it yet.
'I am not sure I can,' she replied. 'It's all very confusing and a bit muddled.'
'Would you like me to make you a cup of tea or maybe something stronger?' Max asked as she opened the door.
'Thank you, yes, that would be good. I think there is a bottle of Granny's scotch in the cupboard, that should

The Garnet Brooch

settle my nerves.'

Max lit the fire, whilst she poured them both a glass of scotch. 'Would you like water with it, or just as it comes?'

'Straight is fine,' he said, taking the glass from her hand and settling down on a cushion in front of the fire. She sipped her drink, its golden warmth spread through her body and she felt herself relax.

'What happened in the churchyard, you looked as white as a sheet when I found you and as though you were far away somewhere?' Max asked.

'I was, it was as if I had gone back fifteen hundred years. I went to sit and unwind after the funeral, it was a bit of a day emotionally and I was worrying about Granny's brooch. I sat there and held it in my hand, it felt like it was getting warm and as I looked around everything became misty. I looked through the mist and I noticed everything had changed, I was back in Saxon times. I saw people coming and going, busy with village life, but they couldn't see me. Then I saw it, Granny's brooch. It was on Queen Ethelburga's cloak. She walked straight past me and down the hill to a large building in the settlement and disappeared from view. People had been calling her name, so I knew it was her. Then I felt your hand on my shoulder and I was back in the present. Perhaps you are right Max, the brooch had belonged to royalty.'

Max was looking at her quizzically, it all seemed a bit fanciful to him, she was probably just overwrought, after all she had been through the last week and the worry of Granny's brooch.

'Don't look at me like that, as though I'm some crazy lady, I know what I saw. It felt so real as though I

could reach out and touch them.'
'Do you think you might have just been over tired, and having the brooch on your mind dreamt the whole thing?'
'No, it happened Max, I know it happened.'
Max poured them another drink and they sat trying to make sense of the whole thing. The warmth of the fire and the scotch made her feel very sleepy.
'Look it's getting late,' said Max, 'I better love you and leave you.'
'Don't go, I need the company, please stay,' she said, placing her hand on Max's arm.
She moved closer to him and laid her head on his shoulder. 'I don't want to be alone.' He felt the warmth of her body and smelt the sweet aroma of her perfume arousing his senses. 'Come on,' he said to himself, 'it's just the whisky, I don't really know her, we only met last week.'
He wasn't thinking, he couldn't be thinking. He just pulled her to him and kissed her full on the lips. Gently at first but as she responded an electric spark ran between them firing his desire. He pulled away and touched her cheek, stroking it softly as he looked into her eyes. 'Do you want me to kiss you again?' he asked.
Max gently drew Erin down onto the cushions by the fire, he couldn't tell whether she was shaking her head yes or no. He had the feeling she didn't know either. 'Erin', he whispered as his lips sought hers once more. He kissed her endlessly, he kissed her tenderly and he kissed her passionately. 'Max' she said, and he lifted his lips from hers, just a bit, just a breath. 'Hmmm.'
'We have to…. Stop.'

The Garnet Brooch

'Mmmmm,' he agreed, but didn't stop. He couldn't, his desire was overwhelming him.

It was madness, complete and utter madness, such wonderful madness.

Max's hand traced the edge of her silk blouse, the first button came easily undone. His kisses crept lower, travelling slowly down her neck as he undid each button, until he revealed a delicate white lace bra. His hand cupped her as he gently kissed her creamy breast causing her to moan with desire. He continued his kisses on their downward journey and proceeded to undo the zip on her skirt. Breaking from their embrace Erin stood up and whispered, 'let's take this upstairs.' Her skirt fell in a pool at her feet and she slowly and seductively removed her blouse, then her bra, until she was standing before him just in her lace briefs. At the top of the stairs she stopped at her bedroom door and looking at him shyly said, 'this is my bedroom.'

He bent down and picked her up in his arms , gently laying her on the bed. His eyes never leaving hers as he took off his shirt and jeans and lay down beside her. Taking her into his arms Max rolled his body over hers. She felt warm and inviting, he could hold back his desire no longer as she quivered beneath him. They made love all night until eventually they fell asleep in each other's arms.

'Morning beautiful, how's the head?' Max said as he came down the stairs.

'Sore,' Erin replied. 'I think we drank that whole bottle of scotch between us.'

She looked up, Max was standing in the stairway in his jeans, nothing else, just his jeans and he looked good, so good she wanted to be in his arms once more.

What was she thinking? Her emotions were getting out of control, things were happening too fast.

She looked beautiful with her long chestnut hair cascading over her shoulders and her big green eyes, looking at him expectantly.

'Don't look so worried, come and give me a good morning kiss,' he said crossing the room. Erin turned and walked to the sink trying to control the feelings she felt inside.

He reached her side and put his hand on her shoulder. She turned and looked into his eyes, resistance was futile, she fell into his arms. They clung to each other and, as her dressing gown came open, she felt his warm chest against her body, soft and strong. Max placed his hands under her arms and lifted onto the kitchen worktop, her legs circling his waist drawing him closer to her. They held each other tight, neither wanting to move and lose the moment, they were in that special place reserved for lovers.

A loud banging on the front door brought them back to reality. They ran upstairs, Erin quickly threw on some clothes and went down to see who it was.

It was Derek, from the dig. 'You seen Max, his jeep's outside so I thought he might be here? We need to open up the church, we've got a group of nuns from Canterbury coming over this afternoon to see what we have uncovered.'

'Yes, come on in, I'll get him, he's upstairs.'

Derek raised an eyebrow, that's how it is, is it, he thought to himself.

Max quickly dressed and hurried downstairs full of apologies as he had completely forgotten the nuns' visit. Usually on a Saturday they had the day off or ran

The Garnet Brooch

guided tours or such like.

'Call you later,' he said, planting a kiss on her lips. He grabbed his phone and jacket and then they were gone.

Erin showered and tidied up from the previous night. She couldn't quite believe how things had turned out. Was it just lust or was she falling in love with this tall dark archaeologist? She still knew very little about him, but somehow it didn't seem to matter.

It had been a long time since she had felt happy, really happy and she smiled and sang to herself as she put things away. Hanging her jacket up she noticed Granny's brooch was missing. It must have fallen off she thought, as she crawled round the floor looking under chairs and tables but found nothing. Where could it have gone? She definitely had it on when she got back last night, she remembered pinning it on to her jacket.

A cold feeling crept over her, he couldn't have done, no, no, no, screamed in her head. She trusted him, she'd shared herself with him, how could he? He must have planned it all, to get his hands on Granny's brooch. What a son of a bitch, a cold calculating son of a bitch and how foolish she was to be taken in by his charm and good looks. 'Why is it that I always pick the wrong men? I am such an idiot', she said to herself. 'When will I ever learn?' Erin sat down and tried to go back over the events of the night before. When they'd got back from the churchyard, she had flung her jacket on the chair and gone to get the scotch. Max was busy preparing the fire and in plain sight. They had been together the rest of the time so he could only have taken it if he'd crept down in the middle of the night.

Not very likely after all that scotch, so how and when did he steal it, and if it wasn't him who else could have done it?

CHAPTER 6

The Year 634

The days were getting longer, and in the hedgerows and fields, snowdrops and narcissi were turning their heads to the sun. Elfin was seven months pregnant now. All through the winter months she had hidden little Alfric, as she called him, beneath the folds of her clothes but it was becoming increasingly more difficult. Several times she had caught Rowena looking at her in a knowing way as she hurriedly dressed in the morning. Elfin prayed daily that it would not be too long now before Alfric returned, if he didn't, she was fearful of what would happen. Her father was a tolerant man, but she was sure he would not be happy with another mouth to feed or with a daughter who was without a husband.

Elfin sat by the fire preparing some leeks for their broth when Rowena appeared with the sackcloth package Alfric had sent her.

'I found this up on the beams whilst I was spring cleaning. Does it belong to you, Elfin?' Rowena asked as she slowly unwrapped it. Elfin was taken by surprise and didn't quite know what to say as the shawl and the garnet brooch were revealed.

Rowena held up the beautiful shawl and stared at the

entwined hearts and letters and turned the brooch over in her hand. 'Is this yours Elfin? Answer me.'

'Yes, they belong to me, they are a gift from my betrothed.'

'Your betrothed, who is the man, is it Bryce, Borward's son? Father has always thought you would marry the son of his dear friend. But wait, the letters are A and E. Who is A?'

'His name is Alfric Huckbone of Apuldre. He was messenger to Queen Ethelburh but has returned to Apuldre to take care of his family and the farm following his father's death. He gave me the parcel and promised to return and make me his own in the spring.'

'That's not all he gave you, by the look of you,' said Rowena, giving Elfin's belly a poke. 'What will Father think, he won't be happy especially as he was planning on your marriage to Bryce?'

'He will like Alfric, he is a good man and he can look after me well. I am sure a good price can be agreed with Father.'

'Do you really think he will return, Elfin? He's had what he wanted and left you for another. Does he know about the baby?'

'No, no I haven't told him.' Elfin replied, tears rolling down her cheeks. 'He loves me, I know he loves me.'

'Not told him? I am sure he will take one look at your belly and take off back home. Loves you? You're a fool, Elfin, believing man's biggest lie of all, just to get what they want.'

'He does love me, he does,' cried Elfin as she kicked the pot of leeks over and ran out of the house and away from Limin.

She didn't know where she was going, she just knew she wanted to find Alfric and be reassured of his love. The road to Apuldre from Limin was a long one across country, dangerous for her with the baby now large in her belly? She had no idea which direction to take or what she should do? In her haste she had left the brooch and shawl behind, perhaps she should go home and get them and ask directions to Apuldre.

Having reached the stream, Elfin crossed over to the wooded copse where she and Alfric had met and sat down under an old oak, to decide the best thing to do.

Rowena was a few years older than Elfin and jealous of her father's favouritism; Elfin always shone the brightest in his eyes. Her arranged marriage to Bryce pierced her to the heart as she had loved him for as long as she could remember and had hoped one day to have him for her own. What would he think of Elfin now with another man's baby in her belly? She put the shawl and brooch on Elfin's bed and continued with her spring cleaning. Sweeping out the dead straw from their bedding and all the dust and dirt that had collected over the winter months. Should she tell Father about Elfin, or leave it for Elfin to tell him? One thing was certain, the baby couldn't be hidden much longer. She prayed for Elfin's lover to return so she could have Bryce as her own.

After finishing the cleaning, she returned to the broth Elfin had been making. It was ruined and she would have to start over – and quickly too, if it was to be ready for lunch. What a waste. Annoyed, she snatched up some more leeks and began to chop them roughly.

Ilfred, their father, would be home soon, hungry from his morning's work in the foundry. Ilfred was the village blacksmith and worked hard making ploughs and weapons as well as horseshoes and pots and pans for the home. He had a good business and made sufficient to meet their needs, bartering with other families for food and cloth. They never went without. What would he think about Elfin? He had always planned that she would marry Bryce. Ilfred and Borward had been friends for a long time and before Dawn his wife had died, they had shaken hands on the agreement. Dawn had died in childbirth a few years after Elfin was born and life had been tough. He had hoped to have a son to carry on the business, but it was not to be. Just the two girls, Rowena and Elfin. Bryce would make a good son in law and take over the business. Now the girls were grown, life had begun to get easier for Ilfred and the future was looking good. He had even turned his thoughts to finding a good woman to share his later years with and the widow Mildred from Paddlesworth had caught his eye more than once, with her comely looks.

'Where's Elfin?' Ilfred asked as he sat down for his midday meal. 'Shouldn't she be doing the cooking today?'

'She went out,' answered Rowena.

'I can see that, where did she go? She's always here for meals, it's not like her.'

'I'm sure she will be home soon, don't worry Father, have your broth whilst it's hot.

When Elfin still hadn't returned by the time Ilfred finished his afternoon's work, they were both worried.

'If you know anything Rowena, tell me. It's getting dark, something might have happened to her.'

Rowena told him the whole story, showing him the brooch and shawl.

'She was very upset and just ran off, I don't know where she went. Maybe to find Alfric?'

Looking at the brooch, Ilfred said: 'this brooch looks valuable, I wonder how he got it. Not something a farmer from Apuldre would usually have. Apuldre is a long walk especially for someone in her condition. I think we should get a search party together to try and find her, anything could have happened. I will go and speak with Borward. He'll know what to do.'

As the sun began to set, Ilfred and the men of Limin went in search of Elfin. Flaming torches held high and dogs barking at their heels.

CHAPTER 7

2019

It had been just over a week since Max had seen Erin. He had knocked on her door every day, and phoned her at least a dozen times, but no answer was her stern reply. It was obvious she was avoiding him since their intimate evening together but why? He thought it had gone rather well, he had enjoyed it very much, much more than he was prepared to admit. Did she regret it? Was she embarrassed? Or had she just decided she didn't like him. She hadn't given him any of those impressions, so what then? He couldn't just leave it, so he decided to sit outside Lavender Cottage and wait. She had to come along sooner or later.

Max was good looking and he knew it. He wasn't used to women turning him down. With him it was usually a one- night stand and then, a goodbye and thank you mam. He'd had his fair share of women and had gotten himself in trouble on numerous occasions especially with angry husbands. He'd managed to use his charm to get out of it on most occasions except for one time when the husband wrote to the University at Reading and told them in no uncertain terms what he thought of one of their staff. From there on the

University made sure he wasn't around long enough to cause trouble and sent him to work on digs in remote locations. Lyminge was his first home assignment in a long time. With Erin he felt different, it was as though they were meant to be together. The attraction was strong and even though he wouldn't admit it something was pulling him, and he didn't want to let her go.

Erin sat in the churchyard. Like Granny she found it soothing to her soul and when she closed her eyes, she felt the stories of the past surround her. Even without the garnet brooch she was taken back to Saxon times, their lives unrolling before her. She felt the connection and knew that she, like Granny, was part of their story. It had been a horrible week, she had managed to avoid Max and ignore his phone calls, but she couldn't help thinking that perhaps she had over reacted. The most sensible thing would be to talk to him, see what he had to say. Yes, she decided, she would talk to Max next opportunity she got.

Erin didn't have to wait long. As she walked down the pathway from the church, she could see his car parked outside the cottage. Taking a deep breath, she walked up to it and tapped on the window. Max was out of the car in a flash.
'Erin, at last,' he said, stepping forward to take her in his arms. 'I've been so worried.'
'You'd better come in,' she said as she turned away from his open arms and walked to the cottage door. They stood staring, waiting for one of them to speak first.

'Well?' Erin finally said.

'Well what. Have I done something wrong? If so, you'd better tell me what, as I have absolutely no idea.'

'Did you take it?'

'Take what? Come on Erin you'll have to give me more than that.'

'Ok. Last Friday, after our evening together, did you take Granny's brooch? Don't lie to me, I know it was there before you left. How could you? I thought I meant something to you after that night, or were you just using me to get what you wanted? What a silly fool I was.'

'Is that what you think of me? Well, thanks, if that's the case you are a silly fool and so am I for thinking we had the start of something good. You disappoint me Erin.'

With that he left, banging the door behind him.

She heard the land rover speed down the road, brakes screeching as he reached the junction, then he was gone.

'That went well,' she said to herself as she sat down on the sofa. 'If it wasn't him, then where would the brooch have gone?' She sat back and closed her eyes for a moment, calming herself . 'Well, she was better off without him, she would be going back to London in a few weeks and would hopefully forget the whole thing.'

She did not sense the silent figure in the corner of the room, watching her from the shadows, the figure which, between one breath and the next, faded into nothing.

Winter was saying farewell and the promise of Spring was just around the corner. Erin couldn't wait until the clocks went forward and the days grew longer, she hated the dark evenings. The wind was getting up and blowing the daffodils to and fro outside the window. Although the day wasn't cold there was an icy chill in the room and Erin shivered. 'Time to light the fire,' she said, as she got up to fetch a basket of logs from the shed. Opening the back door, she stepped away from the shelter of the house and felt the push of the wind, as it furiously tugged at her hair. Grabbing the logs, she ran back indoors, breathless and cold. A strange smell came from the kitchen, a sweet musty sort of scent, earthy. It hadn't been there before, Erin was sure. Perhaps it was the logs.

With the fire burning brightly in the hearth, Erin sat cuddling a warm cup of soup. The room still felt icy though, and the strange smell seemed to be getting stronger. Was she imagining it or was there someone in the room, she could feel an unfamiliar presence? She looked round the room, 'Is there anyone there?' she said into the silence.

Not a murmur came from the pale lips of the intruder standing in the corner. Silent and still, grey eyes unblinking, golden hair dulled by the darkness. One minute she was there, her eyes fixed on Erin holding her in their gaze, then the next she slowly faded into the shadows. 'Is there anyone there?' Erin asked again, but all was silent.

In need of some company, Erin decided to go to the Coach and Horses for a large glass of wine and a chat to Jo. He always had a yarn or two to share. As she crossed the road, the pub sign swung precariously in the wind. Warm lights from the pub were welcoming and she could hear the raucous laughter from alcohol infused customers.

'How's my favourite girl?' he asked with a wink.

'Not having a good day Jo. I need cheering up. Made a fool of myself over Max and lost Granny's brooch. Now I am hearing things in the cottage and there is the most dreadful smell which seems to be getting stronger.'

'Lost the brooch you say? I'll keep my eyes and nose to the ground, if I find out anything, I'll let you know. I'd be surprised if Max took it, he seems an honest sort of chap, and anything to do with the dig he always takes straight to the University lot at Canterbury.'

'Thing is Jo, if he didn't take it, where did it go?'

'Don't be too quick to judge, is all I can say.'

The wine slid down nicely, warming her inside and relaxing her. Erin sat sipping her drink watching all the comings and goings in the pub. It was doing well, Jo had really done a good job with the refurbishments and new bar menu. The wooden tables and chairs had been replaced with leather padded benches and round tables which felt warm and welcoming. All the old brown paint work and cigarette stained walls had been given a fresh coat of pastel blue and white giving the whole place a clean fresh feeling.

The original fireplace and fittings accumulated over the years stood as a reminder of years past, giving it that olde worlde atmosphere. But it was mainly Jo and his wife Hetty who made the place with their good humour and tasty food. A good community centre for young and old. The pub was busy that evening and it was a while before Jo came back for another chat.

'Another?' he asked, taking her glass and refilling it before she had time to answer.

'Did your Granny ever tell you about the woman who is said to haunt Lavender Cottage?'

'I don't remember anything Jo, do tell.'

'They say that a young Saxon woman's spirit roamed Lyminge looking for a brooch given to her by her beloved. She found it in a shallow grave near your Granny's house. Knowing that the brooch is safe, she is able to rest in peace, and happily keeps silent watch in the shadows, every so often appearing to those who live there. However, if the brooch should ever go missing, she swore she would take her revenge. Perhaps the story is true and now that the brooch has gone missing, her spirit has been awakened.'

Erin took a large gulp of her wine. 'Bloomin' heck Jo, do you really think so? But why the bad smell, a coincidence maybe? This whole thing is beginning to sound crazy, I think I need another drink.'

A few more wines down the road, Erin walked unsteadily back to Lavender Cottage. Opening the door, she was hit once again by the strange smell. 'It could be a dead mouse or something under a cupboard,' she thought as she threw off her coat and went upstairs. She'd worry about that tomorrow, bed was calling.

Erin had always been afraid of the dark as a child and with all the strange goings on over the last few days those old feelings were coming back. She felt jittery, unsettled and on edge all the time. As a child, night after night she would lie awake, not daring to move, hardly daring to breathe, her eyes darting here and there around the room, looking for goodness knows what. There was never anything there, nothing frightening. Just an overwhelming feeling of loneliness, and a fear that everyone had left the house and abandoned her. It started after her parents' accident, and so dear Granny had bought her a beautiful crystal angel to guard her as she slept. Its large wings spread ready to cover her with their feathers and keep her from all harm. It was lit by a small t-light which glowed warmly making her feel loved. Over the years it had given her great comfort and she still kept it by her bedside. As she sat on the bed, she lit the tiny candle and with her guardian angel watching her she slipped into a dreamless sleep.

Opening one eye she noticed the t-light had gone out and shafts of daylight shone around the curtains. She guessed it must be around seven o'clock. Her head was killing her, and she quickly shut her eyes. 'How many glasses did I have last night? Ouch!' She rolled over and hid her head under the covers and slowly drifted back to sleep.

She awoke with a start; her bedroom felt very cold. Then she heard it, a voice, a voice she had heard before. Chills ran down her spine and prickles rose on the back of her neck.

'Find the truth and set me free, my story will reveal the key. Give me my life that I can sing a new song, rewrite the past and remove all that is wrong. Hold the brooch within your heart,

never let it from you depart. It is rightfully yours and not for the taking, after the setting of the sun a new dawn is breaking.'

CHAPTER 8

The Year 634

After resting under the trees in the glen by the stream Elfin began the long walk to Apuldre. It was growing dark and she was getting weary. She would have to find herself a place to rest for the night soon. Heading up over the knoll past the Thane's store house, she was suddenly hit by a strong cramp-like pain in her belly causing her to bend over. It was too soon for the baby, she thought to herself, and taking a deep breath straightened up to continue on her path. She had only gone a few steps when another pain came, ripping through her body and taking her breath away. A warm wet feeling ran down her legs as the baby's waters broke. Elfin cried out in pain and sank down on the stony path before her. 'Help!' she cried aloud into the darkness. 'I can't have my baby now. He can't arrive yet, it is too soon.' As another pain took hold, Elfin screamed digging her nails into the stones. She must have passed out because the next thing she was aware of was a monk leaning over her.

'Wake up, my child, wake up,' he said as he patted her face. Another contraction began, and Elfin was fully awake. The monk realising what was happening, scooped her up in his arms and walked back towards the monastery. There was a community of sisters there. They would know what to do.

He was right – the nuns knew exactly what to do. They laid her on a bed of straw and all through the night tended to her needs as best they could. They gave her a stick to bite on as the pains came thick and fast, washing her face with a damp cloth and giving her sips of water from a wooden cup. As dawn broke Elfin's urge to push came like a rushing wind. She pushed with all her might and just as it looked like all was lost, baby was born. The nuns cleaned him up and wrapped him in Elfin's shawl and laid him in her arms.

'You have a healthy son my child, God be praised. Rest now. We'll come back with some refreshment shortly.'

A while later the sound of footsteps aroused Elfin from her slumber as the nuns arrived bringing warm bread and mead.

'I don't know how to thank you.' She tried to sit up. 'You've been so kind.'

'Now don't you fret, have some food and regain your strength and then we'll talk,' said the nun who seemed to be in charge. As she spoke the other nuns busied themselves, cleaning up, bringing Elfin some clean clothes and swaddling cloth for the baby.

Elfin was still in shock. She hadn't thought that baby was due until later in the spring. Perhaps it was all the upset with Rowena that had brought him early. As she stroked his little head, she wondered how she could get word to Alfric, let him know he was a father. The morning passed peacefully and feeling refreshed from the bread and mead, she cleaned herself and dressed in the fresh clothes the nuns had provided.

As the days passed and her strength began to return and while Alfric was fussed over by the adoring nuns, Elfin busied herself helping the nuns with their daily chores. She wanted to pay them back for their kindness, resolving to sweep the refectory and wash the plates. Polish the silver candlesticks and icons, in fact do whatever she could to help.

Two weeks went by. Life was peaceful in the monastery, but she knew she could not hide there forever. She would have to face her father and trust he would be understanding and maybe even take her to Apuldre in his cart to find Alfric. Alfric wouldn't abandon her she was sure, to her his love was real and she loved him with all her heart. She prayed to the Virgin Mary that her father would not reject her and that when they found Alfric they would be married, then together with the baby, they would all live happily as a family. Elfin hoped as a mother the Virgin Mary would be merciful and intercede to God on her behalf.

It was approaching the time for morning prayers and Elfin awoke to a great commotion outside the dormitories.

'Where's my wife?' boomed a deep gruff voice. 'What have you done with her? I want to see her at once.'

Then another voice, one she remembered well. It was her father.

'Take us to my daughter Elfin. We know she is here.'

The door burst open and in strode her father together with a big hulk of a man that she recognised as Bryce, her father's best friend's son. All was silent as they entered the room and took in the sight before them of

Elfin and the baby Alfric nursing at her breast, until the startled baby broke the silence by his cry.

CHAPTER 9

2019

Her lover calls her.
'I am here, my beloved,' she answers.
'Yours for eternity, bound by the garnet brooch.'
'Let not it be taken from its rightful place or I will return
and claim what is ours,' Alfric replies.

Erin felt awful, her head ached , her eyes were sore, and she felt thoroughly sick. She guessed she must have picked up some bug or other, but she couldn't shake it off. The smell in the cottage didn't help and to make matters worse, a coating of what looked like ash covered the floors and furniture, even permeating into the cupboards and fridge. She couldn't think, her head was all of a muddle, perhaps some fresh air might do her good. Trying to muster up some energy, she pulled on her boots and coat and made her way out of the door and up towards the church. The dig had finished, and they had started packing up. There was no one about so she walked up to Granny's seat and sat and looked over the churchyard.

Unlike before there was no going back in time, no nuns and no Queen Ethelburga. The fresh air was doing her good and her head began to clear. The last week had gone past in a blur. Whatever was ailing her had made her lose all sense of time. She had heard nothing from Max, but then she couldn't really blame him as she had accused him of stealing Granny's brooch. If it wasn't him, then who? Should she go to the police? She didn't know what to do or where to start. She sat for a good hour listening to the birdsong all around her, enjoying the peace and quiet of the churchyard and the views over the fields. Feeling refreshed she made her way to the Coach and Horses for a large glass of wine and a chat with Jo. He might have some news, and he always made her feel better.

'Good to see you, Miss Erin. We had been wondering where you were, not seen you out and about for over a week now.'
'I've had the flu or something like it and haven't felt up to doing anything,' Erin replied, as she picked up her large glass of Merlot. Jo always knew what she wanted before she opened her mouth.
'That'll do you a power of good, drink up and I'll pour you another. Just got to bring a barrel up from the cellar and I'll join you for a chat. Got some news.'

Jo had been the publican at the Coach for a good few years. He loved the village and its eclectic mix of people. He and Hetty made a good living, especially with his little business on the side. He wasn't sure how he'd fare now after Brexit. All the new rules and regs and increased tax duty wouldn't make it worthwhile. The duty-free wine and spirits had been a good little earner along with cigarettes and tobacco. His mate Bill went once a month to France and filled up his camper

The Garnet Brooch

with as much as he could fit in. Jo would sell it and they would share the profits. He was ok as long as Hetty and the brewery didn't find out. They wouldn't be too pleased. So it was his and Bill's little secret. Bill was doing a drop today, after hours as always. And under the cover of darkness. Jo just needed to open the side door down to the cellars and Bill would stash it around the back.

The wine began to revive her, and she felt better than she had all week. She wondered about treating herself to the day's special, 'Chilli con Carne'. Her appetite was returning.

Jo strolled over with his half of Guinness and sat next to her at the bar.

'I was going to pop over and tell you, but you beat me to it. The dig was in here the other night, not Max, haven't seen him for a while but old big mouth Derek was bragging to the group that he had made a substantial find that was going to make him a fortune. He wasn't prepared to say what, but my guess is that it could be your brooch.'

'Derek, of course, Derek, why didn't I think of him before? He had the opportunity whilst Max and I were upstairs. How stupid was I blaming Max, no wonder he walked out on me?'

'Sounds as though you have some making up to do. I wouldn't leave it too late though if I were you, I've heard now the dig is finished he's on his way back to Reading.'

'Thanks Jo I'll give him a call . Now how about a plate of your Chilli con carne? I'm famished.' Erin picked up her mobile and punched in Max's number. He didn't pick up. She left a message and sat sipping her wine, thinking over what Jo had told her. Hopefully Max would know how to contact Derek and have some idea of how to challenge him. That's if he forgave her of course.

It was a beautiful evening, the sky a blanket of stars, the moon shining brightly overhead and a magical glow lighting Erin's path home. Feeling revitalised, Erin opened her front door and hung up her coat. Almost immediately she felt a spirit of heaviness press down on her and a feeling of fear and unease. Was there someone there? She looked around, was that someone standing in the corner, hidden by the shadows?
Her throat was tight and her voice very husky. 'Is there anyone there?' she called into the darkness. No one answered. She reached for the light switch, but nothing happened, the lights weren't working. Stumbling around the furniture, she made her way to the log burner in search of some matches, but every time she struck one it blew out. What was going on? She made her way back to the front door, but it wouldn't open. Erin was getting scared now and went to try the back door and the windows. They were the same. The strange smell was getting stronger, almost overpowering, making her feel light headed and woozy. Clutching the chair for support she found she had begun to shake, and her knees felt about to give way. Then she was enveloped in a cloud of darkness as all slipped away .

Max stared at the message on his phone. Erin. He

wasn't sure he wanted to answer. She'd hurt him, accusing him of stealing the garnet brooch. He wasn't ready to forgive.

He had tried to put her out of his mind, move on, go home and forget all about her but it wasn't working. Every day as he drove past the cottage on the way to the dig, he was reminded of their night together. Of her soft skin, warm and inviting lips, her gentle caresses. It was driving him crazy. Looking at the finds from the dig reminded him of the brooch. Just thinking about it filled his mind with strange thoughts and feelings. He must have the brooch, it belonged to him and so did Erin. It was as though it was drawing him in, taking control of his mind. What was the matter with him? It was only a brooch.

How could Erin think he'd steal it? He thought his actions showed she could trust him, but obviously not. His pride was hurt, but more than that his heart felt torn apart. Unwittingly he had fallen in love, dammit. His finger hovered over the message. Should he pick it up and risk being hurt more or live wondering what she wanted? He clicked on the message and his screen lit up.

'Max I am so sorry, so very sorry, I know it wasn't you who took the brooch, I hope you will forgive me and phone me back and let me make it up to you. Please call. Love Erin xx'

CHAPTER 10

The Year 634

Elfin looked up as Rowena entered the room. She had been home a month now. Life was going on as usual, cooking, cleaning, fetching the water but now of course there was baby Alfric to look after. Father hadn't said much since she'd been home except to state that she and Bryce would be married at summer solstice, when the sun was at its highest and the day at its longest. She had tried to talk to him, tell him about Alfric but he wouldn't listen. It had been agreed that she would marry Bryce since she was born, he would not go back on his word. Bryce was prepared to forgive her foolishness with Alfric, accusing him of taking advantage of an innocent woman. Her father told her she was a very lucky girl that Bryce would still have her and to obey her father and her husband. There was no more to be said.

Rowena however was more understanding; she saw what went on and heard secrets that the men shared.

When Elfin ran away, Father had searched the house for clues to where she might have gone and had found her shawl and the garnet brooch. He had given the shawl back to her for the baby. The brooch, however, he had taken for himself, promising it to Bryce on their wedding day.

'Would you like me to mind baby Alfric whilst you bathe? It's warm today and you should find it pleasant in the stream?' asked Rowena.

A stranger had been in the village asking about Elfin, a stranger from Apuldre. Rowena hoped the stranger might be the baby's father come to claim her sister, so she had got word to him to meet Elfin at the stream that afternoon.

'You are kind to me, dear sister. Thank you, I'll go now before Father is back for his meal.'

Elfin hadn't been down to the stream since she'd had Alfric and it was very pleasant sitting with her feet dangling in the water. She was lost in her thoughts when she felt a tap on her shoulder. Looking up she found she was staring at the messenger who had brought Alfric's message to her. She jumped up in surprise looking from left to right to see if he was with Alfric, but he was alone.

'Do you have news for me Sire?' Elfin asked. 'News of my love Alfric?'

'Alfric has heard news that you are to marry Bryce of Limin, and that you have a child. As the promise is broken between you, he would like the garnet brooch returned to him, I am not to return without it.'

Elfin stood in a daze. 'I do not have the brooch. My father has taken it and is going to use it to pay Bryce to take me as his wife.'

'And why would he need to do that if you have the man's child? The brooch is not yours, it belongs to Alfric Huckbone, of Apuldre.'

'But Sire, my child is Alfric's.' Elfin looked round,

The Garnet Brooch

anxious about eavesdroppers, and lowered her voice. 'It is his son, not Bryce's.'

'This is only what you say, can it be proved? I will speak with your father.'

The messenger from Aldington followed Elfin back home. Her father was standing outside talking to Borward. They turned to stare at the stranger as he approached.

'Elfin, who is this stranger that you bring to our home?' he asked.

'My name is Edwin, cousin to Alfric Huckbone of Apuldre. I am here to collect the garnet brooch which is rightfully his.'

'Rightfully his, rightfully his?' Ilfred shouted. 'This Alfric gives it to my daughter as payment for her favours, leaves her with a baby in her belly and then has the nerve to ask for it back. I am insulted that you think me so stupid. The brooch is now mine and it will be Elfin's dowry when she marries Bryce.'

'The brooch was given to Elfin, as a love token, a sign of Alfric's fidelity and promise to marry. It doesn't belong to you and Alfric is entitled to its return as the promise is broken.'

Elfin stood between the two men and raised her arms, 'Stop, stop this, take me and the baby to Alfric and I will settle the matter. Father, please give me the brooch.'

'Take the baby but Elfin and the brooch stay. That is my final word. Rowena, bring out the child.'

Rowena appeared in the doorway with baby Alfric in her arms. 'You called, Father?'

'Give the baby to this man and let's be done with it. Take it and leave now or I will set my men on you.'

Edwin looked at the baby thrust into his arms. Blonde curls framed his little face and the greenest of eyes looked up at him, there was no doubt Alfric was the father.

'No, Father, please, don't let him take my baby,' Elfin cried. 'Father I beg you.'

'You haven't heard the last of this, Ilfred. My cousin and I will return, and he will not be put off from taking that which is his. I bid you farewell.'

With that, Edwin turned, mounted his horse and with baby Alfric tucked in the crook of his arm, galloped off in the direction of Apuldre.

CHAPTER 11

2019

Erin opened her eyes. They felt gritty as though someone had thrown sand in her face. Pulling herself out of the chair she headed towards the kitchen in need of a hot drink. The room was so cold, and she felt very wobbly. What happened just then, she wondered?

Max, having tried to call Erin, decided to go to the cottage and see if she was home.
Her car was outside but there was no answer at the door, so he decided to go over to the Coach and Horses and see if she was there. Jo might know where she was.
As he went to leave, he noticed a strange smell, like rotting flesh and saw ash coming from under the front door. In fact, the cottage looked grey, as though it were dying. He renewed his knocking on the door. 'Erin, Erin? Are you in there? It's me Max, open the door.' Something strange was going on. He was sure she was in there.
As the kettle boiled, Erin thought she heard banging. Her attention, however, was drawn to a swarm of angry flies buzzing around the light switch and

bouncing off the ceiling. 'Where had they come from? They weren't here earlier.' There was dirt everywhere, on the floor, in the cupboards, on the worktop and even in the sink. As she stared into the bowl her stomach lurched as she saw a pile of wriggling maggots in the filth that lay there. The smell seemed to be getting worse, more intense and she felt as though she was going to be sick.

The banging was getting louder and louder. Eventually she realised someone was knocking on her door. She walked nervously towards it and this time it opened with no problem.

'Erin, thank goodness. My God, what's happened to you, you're covered in ash and as white as a ghost?'

'Oh Max.' Her tears turned to sobs as she fell into his arms. 'I don't know what's going on. Everything's out of control, and I am sure someone is in the cottage. They locked me in.'

'It's ok, I'm here now Erin, let's have a look round.'

As they went back into the cottage, the first thing they saw written on the wall in ash was:

'Bryce Borson, May the gods of all eternity curse you.'

As they stood staring, a gust of wind blew in shutting the door with a bang. Inside the cottage all had gone back to normal, no ash and no smell, and the message was gone. If Max hadn't seen it with his own eyes, he would have never believed it.

'What's been going on, Erin, and who the hell is Bryce Borson?' he asked.

'I've never heard of him,' Erin replied. 'I'd not been feeling too good, I had a touch of flu or something and I went out for some fresh air. There had been a strange smell and I felt a presence in the cottage. It

The Garnet Brooch

began to make me feel sick. After a little walk in the churchyard, I felt a bit better, so I went to the Coach for a glass of wine.'

She went through to the kitchen and put the kettle on.

'Jo told me about a story Granny had told, of a young Saxon girl whose spirit roamed Lyminge looking for a brooch given to her by her lover. She found it in a grave where Lavender Cottage now stands. Provided it's safe, she rests in peace. If the brooch is stolen or goes missing, she has sworn to take her revenge.

When I got home the atmosphere felt heavy and I thought there was someone in the cottage. I called out but no one answered. I reached for the light switch, but the lights didn't work, the doors wouldn't open, and the windows were locked. The smell was getting stronger and I must have passed out.'

'When I arrived,' said Max, 'I knocked and knocked on the door and nearly went home, except I felt something was wrong. I'm so glad I stayed.'

He took her in his arms and gave her another big hug as she continued with the story.

'When I came to, the cottage looked such a mess. There was dirt and ash everywhere. Flies were buzzing around the light in the kitchen and there were maggots in the sink. I don't know where it's come from. All the time I felt as though someone was watching me, I think they were looking for something, do you think it was the brooch? This all started when the brooch went missing.'

'It's all very peculiar, If I didn't know better, I would think you're being haunted.'

'I think we need something stronger than tea,' said Max, heading for Granny's stash of whisky.

The Garnet Brooch

They sat down with their two large tumblers full.

'You remember what happened the last time?' said Erin letting the amber liquid warm her inside and out and begin to steady her nerves.

Max smiled, 'I'll light the log burner. It feels like someone has walked across my grave, if you'll excuse the pun.'

It was so good to see Max. She had missed him so much and all because of her own stupidity. 'You got my message?' she asked shyly. 'I'm so sorry, I shouldn't have jumped to conclusions.'

'You hurt me Erin, I thought we meant something to each other. I thought you could have trusted me.'

'I should have done, I was a fool. Please forgive me and let me make it up to you.'

Max looked at her, giving her a sultry look under sex-filled eyes.

'How about making it up to me now? It may take a long time, you hurt me a lot.' he replied as he took her in his arms and kissed her slowly and gently.

Erin melted into his arms and as his kisses grew more passionate, the spark between them ignited their desire.

'Do you think we should see if there is anyone in the cottage? Someone may be watching us,' said Erin.

'Good, I've never been watched by a ghost before,' he replied as he took hold of her waist and ran his hands up her sides, lifting the edge of her jumper pulling it over her head. Drawing her closer he sought the zip of her skirt and seductively lowered it until her skirt fell to the ground. She pulled open his shirt and ran her hands over his toned body. 'God, you turn me on,' she said as he laid her down on the rug. 'Make love to me

Max, I want you so much.'

'No, I think I'll make you wait, your penance for upsetting me,' came his reply as he stared down at her. He took her wrists and placed them over her head as he kissed the top of her breasts and gently pressed kisses down her torso, over her stomach to the top of her panties. Keeping her arms held over her head he traced his fingers along the top of her panties making her squirm with longing.

'Max please,' she cried as he came near to her precious area of delight.

'What do you want Erin?' he teased. 'Do you want me, really want me?'

He stood up and removed his jeans. 'Tell me Erin, tell me you want me.'

Their love making was fierce and passionate, each holding on to every moment and giving everything until nothing was left. Then when all was done, he took her again slowly and lovingly, their lust replaced by the love they felt for each other.

Max didn't know how long he had lain there with Erin snuggled up beside him, but his right arm had gone dead and he was freezing. She was sleeping peacefully now after what he could only call her unearthly experience. If he hadn't seen it with his own eyes, he would have thought it was all in her mind but there was no getting away from that message on the wall. All that dust and the smell…He wasn't sure what to make of it, but he was as sure as hell going to find out. Was someone trying to frighten Erin off, send her running back to London? Then with her out of the way claim the brooch as their own? Releasing his numb arm from underneath her, he lifted her up gently and climbed the stairs to her bedroom. Laying her down on the bed he placed the duvet over her and went downstairs to think.

The first light of day was visible through the curtains when he felt an icy chill sweep over him. As he stood to get a jacket, he thought he saw someone standing in the corner of the room. It seemed to float in and out of the shadows. 'Is there anyone there?' he said into the darkness but as he approached whoever it was disappeared.

Then he heard it. It was very quiet at first and then grew stronger, a voice, a woman's voice.

'Bryce Borson may the gods of all eternity curse you and bring your putrid body and your rotten soul to judgement for what you have done.'

Then silence. Where had that come from, was he hearing things now? First the message on the wall and now the voice. Who was Bryce Borson?

Picking up the poker from the fire grate, he looked in all the corners, behind the doors and even in the cupboards but nothing. 'This is madness,' he said to himself as he sat down on the sofa. Closing his eyes, he went through the facts.

1. The brooch has been taken and since then a spirit from the past has been disturbed.

2. We need to find the story of the brooch to prove who it belongs to.

3. When the brooch is restored to its rightful owner, the spirit will be at peace.

There was another question which troubled him –

who was Bryce Borson? Did he take the brooch?

'So, it really is all about the brooch,' he murmured. He could see it in his mind's eye, he could see it on a golden cloak, the red garnets sparkling in the sunlight, so close he could almost touch it. It called to him, and he reached out to take it, but then it was gone, disappearing into the ether.

He must have dozed off, and as he awoke, he could smell the sweet aroma of coffee. Opening his eyes, Erin was standing over him with two cups of coffee in her hand. 'Morning, handsome.' she said with a smile.

CHAPTER 12

The Year 634

There was a thundering of hooves, it could be heard throughout the village.

At least half a dozen men dressed ready for battle came to a stop outside Elfin's home.

'Where is she, where is Elfin, the mother of my child?' came a loud cry. 'I come to claim that which is mine, I am Alfric Huckbone of Apuldre. I will not be put off.'

Roused from his bed, Ilfred appeared in the doorway looking very surprised.

'Sire,' he said, 'come and sit a while and we can talk this through. Can I offer you some warm mead?' Turning towards the door he shouted, 'Rowena, Rowena get yourself up and bring these men some refreshment.'

A sleepy Rowena came out followed by Elfin. She ran up to Alfric and he lifted her into his arms and onto his horse.

'Now bring me my brooch and I will leave,' Alfric bellowed.

'The brooch is rightfully mine, as a dowry for Elfin.'

The Garnet Brooch

said Ilfred. 'We have made no agreement for marriage, so it stays with me.'

'Elfin will be my wife, she has borne my son. Bring me the brooch.'

All the noise and commotion had woken Bryce and his father Borward. Bryce approached Alfric and his men.

'You cannot scare us with your shouting and these men dressed for battle. Elfin is to be my wife, it has been agreed from our birth,' Bryce said, as he went to take Elfin from Alfric's arms.

Elfin clung tightly on to Alfric.

'The brooch belongs to Alfric. He gave it to me as a sign of our betrothal. It is not Father's to give you, Bryce, and I will choose whom I marry.'

Alfric stared at Bryce. 'You care only for one thing. The brooch. You care nothing for Elfin. You only want to marry her for the brooch and the riches you believe it will bring you.'

'The brooch, the brooch,' Bryce replied. 'Where did a simple farmer like you get such a valuable brooch, did you steal it?'

'It was a gift from our Queen Ethelburh. I have stolen nothing.'

'A gift, why would she give you a gift? Let us go to the royal residence. The Queen will prove you to be a liar and a cheat.'

A large crowd encircled Alfric and his men and led them to the royal residence. When they arrived, Alfric spoke to the guard and asked to have an audience with Queen Ethelburh. They needed to settle a dispute.

The Queen had seen the crowd approaching and was

The Garnet Brooch

ready to meet them. She immediately saw Alfric and went to greet him, taking his hand as he fell on his knees before her. Bryce stood behind him and as he offered his hand, she turned away and walked on with Alfric and Elfin. Bryce burned with the humiliation.

'Where is my garnet brooch?' asked Queen Ethelburh.

'Ilfred Smithson of Limin has it, your majesty. I gave it as a sign of my betrothal to his daughter Elfin and he has taken it and promised it to Bryce Borson as a dowry on their marriage.'

'Elfin, who will you choose as your husband, Bryce Borson or Alfric Huckbone?' asked the Queen.

'I love Alfric, your majesty, and we have a baby son. I only wish to marry him, I belong to no other. My father is wrong to keep the brooch, it belongs to Alfric.'

'I know the brooch belongs to Alfric, it is I who gave it to him. Alfric worked for many years as my loyal and trusted messenger. When his father died, and he returned to Apuldre, I gave him the brooch in thanks for all his service. Where is this Ilfred Smithson?'

'Here my lady.'

'Return the brooch at once to Alfric of Apuldre. May it be a blessing on his marriage to your daughter Elfin. This is my will.'

Bryce was angry. Although he had been promised to Elfin from birth, it was the thought of losing the brooch and the riches it would bring when they married that really upset him. Alfric's comment had touched a nerve.

'Elfin has been promised to me,' he roared, 'I demand that this is settled in the old way. We fight tomorrow at daybreak.'

'If Alfric loses the battle, the brooch will be returned to me. You will not gain by this action,' responded the Queen.

'I want satisfaction. Alfric, I call you out. Tomorrow at dawn'.

'Tomorrow at dawn, it will be,' said Alfric.

The Queen's ladies took Elfin and dressed her in fine clothes, brushed her hair until it shone and decorated it with spring flowers. The tables were spread with luscious foods, a roasted pig and a fine goose, and in the centre of the room a deer on a spit. Fruits and fresh bread for all, washed down with the finest of ales and mead.

There was singing and dancing and the whole village were invited to celebrate the marriage of Elfin and Alfric. Whilst the feasting and merrymaking continued into the night Alfric and Elfin slipped away to the shelter of the trees. Kisses denied them for so long were hot and passionate and they held onto each other, frightened that the moment would be stolen from them.

'Forgive me, my darling, I should have come for you sooner. Since father died my life has not been my own as I have been called upon to take care of the family and the farm.'

'I prayed for you to return every day. To return before baby Alfric was born but Rowena found the brooch and shawl and our secret was revealed. I didn't know what to do, so I decided to come and find you, but my journey was cut short when my pains started. I was lucky that one of the monks found me and took me to the nuns at the monastery, where they looked after me until little Alfric was born. They were so kind.'

'My poor love, you must have been very frightened, if only I'd known. I am here now, and I will never let you go again. Lc lufie be, Elfin.' Bryce stood in the shadows waiting for the sun to rise. He would get his revenge and have Elfin and the brooch for himself.

CHAPTER 13

2019

'I watch you from the shadows. I know what you do, the truth cannot be hidden.'

Max's phone beeped, it was a message. A message from the digs director at Reading.
'Bad news Max, phone me asap. Roley'
'I wonder what that's all about, sounds serious.'
Erin was snuggled up in Max's arms on the sofa under a warm blanket, her second cup of coffee of the morning in her hand.
'What's up, problems with the dig?' she asked.
'I better call the University, I'll be back in a minute,' Max replied as he slipped his jacket on and went out into the back garden.
Erin looked round the room, everything looked normal this morning, no ash, no funny smell. Had she imagined it all? No, Max had experienced it too. Maybe the ghost Jo had told her about was true. She didn't believe in ghosts, what was she thinking, but what else could it be? Perhaps she and Max should go over to the Coach and Horses and have a chat with Jo. It was a place to start at least, to get to the bottom of this mystery. Max thought it was all connected to

Granny's brooch and maybe it was. Things had started happening after it was lost.

Max appeared in the doorway with a look of disbelief on his face.

'That call was about Derek, he's dead. He was on his way to visit his parents in Swindon when his motorbike spun off the road into the central reservation. The guy in the car behind him said he couldn't understand it. He wasn't speeding, the road was clear ahead and there was nothing on the road to cause him to spin off. It was all very strange. It was as though someone or something had pushed him.'

'How dreadful, poor Derek. I didn't like him, but I would never have wished that on him. His family will be devastated.'

'That's not all of it,' said Max. ' Apparently when they removed his crash helmet it was full of powder, like ash.'

They stood looking at each other. The room felt cold and damp although the fire was still burning, and the strange smell had returned. Erin felt a cold shiver down her spine and turned her head as she felt someone was behind her.

'Who are you, what do you want, show yourself?' she shouted into the corner of the room. It was shrouded in darkness and for a moment Erin thought she glimpsed a figure, but then it faded and returned to the shadows. Gradually the smell disappeared, and the room felt warm once more and things returned to normal.

Max shook his head. 'I don't know what's happening here, but we need to find out. It all has something to do with the garnet brooch, I'm sure. If we find the brooch and reveal its story, we will find the answers. Let's pop over to the Coach.'

They sat drinks, in hand at the bar in the Coach and Horses. Erin had her usual large glass of Merlot, but Max had a double brandy. He needed it after the morning's events. They'd hoped to talk to Jo, but he'd gone to do the weekend's banking, so they sat and chatted to Hetty.

Hetty knew all about the ghost of Lavender Cottage. Apparently, Hilda had chatted about it all the time. She'd told them it was a young Saxon girl who had been crossed in love. The garnet brooch had been a love token and it was said that if it ever left the family the young woman's heart would break and she would be separated forever from her one true love. A curse was on anyone who took it, removed it from its ancestral home, a curse of death.

'Your Granny wore the brooch at all times,' Hetty went on, as she deftly polished a box of pint glasses. 'It never left her side, she felt she was part of its story.'

'I wish she was here now,' Erin sighed. 'She could explain it all to us.'

Jo returned from the bank and joined them at the bar.

'You were a long time Jo, any problems?' asked Hetty.

'Oh, I just popped round to see Bill, I wanted to borrow his strimmer. That honeysuckle round the trellis needs a good trim,' Jo replied, innocently. .

'Hello Erin, Max, are you still having trouble with the ghost?' Jo asked with a chuckle.

'Don't laugh Jo,' replied Erin. She proceeded to tell him all that had been going on over the last few days.

'Sounds as though all your troubles stem from losing the brooch. Any luck finding it? Have you tried that Derek fella? I told you he'd been in here last week boasting about something he'd found that was going to make him a lot of money?'

'Derek's dead,' said Max. 'Under very suspicious circumstances. He came off his motorbike on the M4. Spun off for no reason, hit the central reservation and broke his neck. The strangest thing was that when they removed his helmet it was full of ash. What do you make of that?'

'Well bugger me,' said Jo. 'It seems we have some pretty weird stuff going on. I think the first thing we need to do is find that brooch.'

Their glasses recharged, they spent the afternoon going over the events of the past week and trying to work out where the brooch might be now. If Derek had it on him, where was it now? His parents might know something or have been given it with Derek's personal possessions. Max decided the best thing he could do was to drive up and see them, offer his condolences and see what he could find out. Meanwhile Erin was going to visit Granny's old friend, Cynthia Baldock. Jo said that if anyone could tell them more about the brooch and the mysterious happenings, it would be Cynthia.

Jo was concerned about Bill. He hadn't shown up with the delivery this week. He was usually very prompt. What if he had got caught by the customs people? They'd both be in for it then. He checked his mobile. Nothing. He tried Bill's number but just got an answerphone message saying, 'this number is unable to

take your call at this time.'
Frustrating, he hated answer phone messages. He'd called round to Bill's in Brady Road on the way back from the bank but neither Bill or Pat his wife was there. Nor was the camper. Where could he have got to?

Cynthia lived in Lyminge, in Mayfield Court, sheltered housing for the elderly, opposite Age Concern on Station Road. She had moved there from Old Robus, a big old house on the way out of the village. It had gotten too big for her now she had reached the grand old age of ninety- seven. A rather eccentric lady who liked to think of herself as a bit of a hippy. She wore her purple hair piled on top of her head, large gypsy earrings, flowing skirts and blouses and an abundance of beads around her neck. She loved to sing and would suddenly burst into song in the middle of a conversation which was quite disconcerting. She also did yoga and you would often find her doing a headstand in the most unusual places.
It was about half past four when Erin knocked on Cynthia's door. She knocked a few times before the door opened to reveal Cynthia in all her glory. Today's ensemble was a very elaborately decorated kaftan in different shades of pink and her hair had been dyed to match in a bright cerise.
'Well I never, it's little Erin Hogden of Lavender Cottage isn't it? What a lovely surprise! Do come in. Let me make you some tea.' She burst into song. 'Tea for two and two for tea, me for you and you for me.'
Erin made herself comfortable on the settee. It was a pretty room full of knick-knacks and photos and

The Garnet Brooch

paintings that Cynthia had done over the years. It was the sort of room that made you smile.

'How are you my lovely? Such a shame Hilda's gone. We went back a long way you know. We first met at school back in the 1930s and grew up together in the village. I shall miss her. We still enjoyed the odd game of bridge and a glass of gin and tonic at the Coach and Horses right up to a few weeks before she passed. Love her.'

'I'm doing okay', replied Erin, 'Of course I miss Granny terribly. She has always been my rock holding my life together.'

She ran a finger over the rim of her teacup.

'Did she ever talk to you about the past? The history of the Hogden family and particularly her garnet brooch?'

'The Hogden family? Yes, she did. She believed the family went back to Saxon times and that her garnet brooch had once belonged to Queen Ethelburga.'

'What about Lavender Cottage, did she talk about a ghost or strange goings on there?'

'Yes, the cottage is said to be haunted by a young Saxon girl and the garnet brooch holds the key. Some say if the brooch does not stay in the Hogden family, then disaster will fall upon all concerned.'

'Did she ever see anyone or smell anything?

'She often said she felt a presence in the house. Shifting shadows that seemed to drift in and out as though they were just checking all was well. She said she found it comforting in a way and would often talk about the young Saxon girl as part of the family.'

'Do you know anything about the history of the brooch or the Hogden family, Cynthia?'

'No not a lot, Hilda's eyes would glaze over when she started talking about the family. Her brother in law, your Great Uncle George Hogden, now he would know. He moved to Faversham way before your time, but I don't know whether he is still alive. Probably not I think he was older than Hilda. A confirmed bachelor and genealogist who loved to dig into local history. I think I have his address somewhere. 'No one to talk with all by myself, no one to walk with, I'm happy on the shelf, ain't misbehavin, saving all my love for you….'

Singing away happily Cynthia scuttled off to the bedroom and began to search through her drawers. As Erin sat sipping her cup of tea, she kept everything crossed that Cynthia would come up with a link to the past. It wasn't long when Cynthia appeared holding a picture frame. It held a photo of Cynthia and Hilda on either side of a very handsome young man in a Naval Uniform.

'This is George, just after he returned from the War. I had a real soft spot for George, but he wasn't interested in me. You can take this if it will help, someone in the village may know his forwarding address, or there might be something in Hilda's papers.'

'Thank you, I'll ask around, maybe Reverend Good will remember him, have something in the church archives.'

Erin went back to the cottage, all seemed normal. She sniffed the air but couldn't smell the horrible smell, nor could she feel a presence in the house. 'I'm going to give this place a good spring clean whilst Max is away, fill the place with flowers and music.'

She put on Granny's pinny and flung wide the windows. She put Michael Buble on the disc player she'd given Granny one Christmas, rolled up her sleeves and made a start on the dusting and hoovering. It was soon done, and Erin flopped down on the sofa, coffee in hand and admired her handiwork. Just then her phone rang, it was Max.

'Hi baby, how did it go with Cynthia this afternoon?'

'I didn't get much, she said more or less what we already know. But she did give me the name of Granny's brother in law. If we can find him, he may know something. How about you?'

'Derek's family were devastated as you'd expect, I didn't stay long, I'm at the University at the moment. But they did say before he drove up to Swindon, he visited Professor Crump in Canterbury to try and get the brooch valued. He left the brooch with him. So, I guess our next move should be to go and see Professor Crump. We need to get the brooch back where it belongs before more things start happening. I'll get a room at the Holiday Inn, then drive back first thing in the morning, should be back just after breakfast. You'll be ok, won't you?'

'All good here, don't worry about me. Have a safe journey my love,' Erin replied.

CHAPTER 14

Year 635

Dawn rose over the valley. In a crescendo of splendour, the sky turned pink with splashes of purple and blue, promising a fine and clear day ahead. The beauty of the sky was overshadowed for Elfin by the thought of her beloved Alfric and his duel with Bryce. How she loved him, and she was so looking forward to spending her life with him and little Alfric in Apuldre. She couldn't lose him now, they had only just found each other again, but it had been agreed. They were to fight on the common this morning, to the death. Alfric unwrapped himself from Elfin's arms and went to find his men who would prepare him for battle. They were good men, they would look after him. He already wore his battle tunic and leggings and the men fitted his iron helmet securely on his head. Weapons were set out on the table for Alfric to make his choice. Choosing carefully, he hung a battle axe from his waist, tucked a dagger into his belt and held his sword firmly in his hand. The sword and dagger were made of iron with ornate handles of bronze and silver, befitting his standing as the Queen's messenger. The shield was his greatest form of protection made of hardened planks of wood fashioned into a large circle, but with edges of sharpened bronze and an iron boss in the centre it also made a very effective weapon. Holding his shield at the ready, Alfric approached the common. He left his men and made his way to the green where Bryce was waiting for him, pacing up and down like a caged animal. Alfric's heart was beating fast in his breast and his hands were wet with fear but he stood tall and strong. He was doing this for Elfin and his newborn son. There was a small crowd of villagers who had come to watch, chanting the names of their favourites. Ilfred, Elfin's father stood before them.

Elfin had crept away from their warm bed and hidden herself in the small copse of trees near the common where she could see clearly all that happened.

'Dear God,' she prayed, 'please keep Alfric safe, keep him from all harm, from the axe and the sword, may the fight be quick and decisive and may neither man suffer. In your mercy God, hear my prayer. Amen.'

Ilfred drew the men into the centre of the large circle that had formed.

'Bryce, Alfric you understand this is a fight to the death and battle will start on my signal. If you start before the signal, I will personally slay the culprit. Is this understood?'

Both nodded their heads in agreement.

'Then prepare yourself for battle.'

Both men stepped away with eyes fixed upon each other. Neither was aware of anything except each other, listening for the signal.

Ilfred cried out, 'Ready, fight.'

With blood curdling roars, Alfric and Bryce charged at one another, axes smashing down on shields, both parrying the blows. Alfric tried a close manoeuvre to quickly end the fight by smashing forward with his shield, but Bryce was ready and fended it away. The crowd was roaring but neither man heard. Bryce raised his axe bringing it down towards Alfric's head but Alfric was too quick and moved to the side taking the blow with his shield. Bringing his own axe in an upwards swoop he smashed Bryce's axe from his hand. Alfric went in for the kill but Bryce swiftly gained his footing and swirled round crashing his shield into Alfric's right arm, knocking the axe from his hand. Both men now drew their swords and once again were confronting each other, face to face. With a flurry of swords, blade against blade, they fought on, their shields protecting them against the onslaught.

The crowd's roar was so deafening that no one heard Elfin's screams from her hiding place. The fighting continued, it felt like an eternity to Elfin, but on and on they fought. They were tiring and their arms were sagging but the shouting and screaming went on and so did the battle. They were now close together, sword against sword, Bryce lunged into Alfric and caught him a glancing blow in his shoulder, throwing him off balance, knocking his shield from his hand as he fell to the ground. He raised his sword in readiness to plunge it into Alfric's heart but Alfric was too quick again, jumping up and thrusting his sword into Bryce's thigh. They fought on with axe and sword, and the battle was fierce. Bryce split Alfric's shield leaving him vulnerable to Bryce's onslaught and as Alfric turned he pulled his axe and threw it at Bryce nearly cutting his arm right

The Garnet Brooch

through. In the chaos Alfric dropped his sword and seeing this Bryce used it to his advantage. With a thundering roar, Bryce grabbed his sword with his good arm and charged at Alfric as he bent to pick up his sword. He struck him hard in his shoulder and as he staggered backwards his arm hung loosely at his side giving Bryce easy access to thrust his sword into his chest. Just as he raised his sword a scream came from the trees as Elfin ran towards Alfric. 'Bryce let him live, I love him, you can have the brooch'.

'Elfin no,' screamed Alfric, as he drew his dagger ready to pierce the unprotected chest of Bryce as he ran at him, but it was too late. Elfin hurled herself forward between the two men trying to stop them but Bryce's sword came down and he plunged it straight through her heart.

The crowd was silent as Ilfred ran to his daughter's side. He picked her up in his arms and rocked her back and forth sobbing. Her blood like a crimson river flowed down his tunic onto the ground where she had died. He turned, his face white in contrast.

'You have done this Bryce with your greed and pride. You have never loved her, I should have seen it. Get out of my sight and out of the village, I never want to see your face again.'

Bryce went to speak, to defend himself but taking one look at the villagers staring at him in horror and disbelief, said nothing.

Bryce's father approached Ilfred as he continued to rock Elfin in his arms.

'Father, I…,' Bryce implored.

'I have no son, my son is dead,' Borward said as he

placed his hand on Ilfred's shoulder. Then together with all the villagers he turned his back on his son.

Bryce looked around for someone, anyone who would speak on his behalf but there was no one. Rowena turned away weeping feeling nothing but loathing for the man she had once loved. There was nothing he could do, so he turned and left, an exile from his village and his family.

Alfric was injured and was being tended to by his men. 'Is Elfin alive?' he managed to say through his pain. 'Tell me she's still alive.'

He struggled to stand and made his way to where Ilfred sat with Elfin in his arms.

'I'm sorry', said Ilfred shaking his head. 'Sorry for all of this. I should have listened to Elfin and not pushed her into marriage with Bryce. I should have believed her when she said she was betrothed . We have both lost today, you, your wife and mother of your child, and me, my daughter. The light has gone out of our lives, today is a day of darkness and grief, we will mourn without ceasing until the sun makes its journey across the moon.'

Through his tears, Alfric declared: 'The garnet brooch will remain as a symbol of our love, I will keep it forever close to my heart and when I die it will be passed from generation to generation. It is always to stay within the Huckbone family. Should the brooch fall into false hands a curse will fall on those concerned, until it is returned. Be warned, I do not give this curse lightly, death and destruction will follow in its wake.'

Elfin was buried just outside the village, on the primrose bank leading up to the church.

The Garnet Brooch

Many mourners came that day, to say goodbye to a young woman, one of their own, taken before her time in such a cruel way. They laid their flowers on her grave and sang songs as they prayed for her spirit to be taken up to heaven. Even Queen Ethelburh came and said prayers at her graveside. Alfric was the last. He did not want to leave her side and knelt for many hours holding the garnet brooch in his hand and whispering words of love. As darkness fell, he placed the brooch inside a small cloth purse, tied with string, and hung it around his neck so it rested just above his heart. Then with one final goodbye he mounted his horse and rode back to Apuldre.

CHAPTER 15

2019

It was just after nine when Max knocked on the door of Lavender Cottage. After a quick coffee they jumped into his land rover and headed for Canterbury. It was a glorious morning. New life was springing up everywhere. The birds were in full voice and primroses adorned the verges as they travelled up Stone Street, discussing their plans and mulling over all they had found out so far.

'The first thing we've got to do is get the garnet brooch back where it belongs, so we don't get any more problems with our Saxon friends,' said Max. 'Let's hope Professor Crump still has it and he hasn't sent it off for valuation.'

They pulled into the University car park at about ten o'clock and headed for Professor Crump's office. When they reached the door, they found it locked with a notice on the door. It read, 'Office closed, due to sickness, please contact Cherry Smithers in the Arts and Humanities Department.'

Cherry Smithers was a lecturer in Arts and Humanities and was also Professor Crump's PA, something of an unofficial role which suited them both and which had started in the days when she was his student. She did everything from making the tea to cleaning and recording new artefacts.

It was one of those days, she thought irritably. Nothing seemed to be going right. She had a splitting headache too. Possibly caused by the horrible smell that had been hanging over the lecture hall, ever since the Professor had been taken ill. It seemed to follow her around, it had got up her nose and down the back of her throat. It was even making her eyes water. She was trying to catch up on the backlog of new arrivals, logging them in, listing them and sending them for cleaning and valuation.

The garnet brooch was one of them. The professor was keen to get it processed and valued as soon as possible, and certainly before there was any interference from the family. Especially Erin Hogden who apparently had some fanciful idea that it belonged to her family. Derek Trott, one of the archaeological team over at Lyminge Church had brought it in saying he had found it at the dig. He had left it with the Professor for authentication and valuation, hoping to get some sort of finder's fee. It was the last thing the Professor had been working on before he collapsed at his desk. He had been fine all day and Cherry had just popped out to get them both a coffee but when she returned, he was slumped over his desk, covered in a fine white dust. He was still alive when the ambulance arrived and took him off to Kent and Canterbury Hospital. She had rung them a few times, but there was no change. He had slipped into a coma and it wasn't looking good. Poor man, he was such a joy to work with and Cherry couldn't think what on earth had happened, or where the ash had come from. All very strange.

As she tidied up the hall after last night's lecture there was a knock at the door.

'Cherry Smithers? My name is Max Judd. I'm the director of the dig at Lyminge Church, I was looking for Professor Crump.'

'I'm sorry he's not here, he's been taken ill, and I don't know when he will be back,' replied Cherry.

'It's important, can you tell me what happened, I need to speak to him urgently?'

Cherry told Max what she knew and said that she didn't know when or if he would return. Turning to Erin, Max put his finger to his lips and gave her a wink. 'Ok I see, do you know where the garnet brooch is that Derek Trott bought in? I need it for the display at Lyminge. We are having an open day to show the public all the items we've excavated.'

'I do have it here. Professor Crump was working on it when he was taken ill but I can't let you have it without proper authority,' answered Cherry.

'When do you think that will be? Is it possible for us to take it for the exhibition and then return it in a week or two? We will take very good care of it and make sure it doesn't get into the wrong hands.' Max gave Cherry one of his best, come and get me smiles.

Cherry blushed and said she would do what she could and let him know. So, having swapped mobile numbers he and Erin left and made their way back to Lavender Cottage.

'Were you giving that Cherry the come on, back there?' Erin asked, as they snuggled up on the sofa.

'I was trying to butter her up a bit, so we would get some preferential treatment,' replied Max. 'Come on, let's forget it all for a while, give us a kiss.'
Max leaned over and kissed Erin gently on the lips, as he drew her into his arms. Before, when he kissed her, his kisses had lit a spark of desire deep within her. This time she felt nothing, his kisses felt cold and empty. She couldn't understand why, but there was nothing there. Perhaps she was just tired or had too much on her mind. Pulling away from his embrace Erin went and put the kettle on. 'I've got an appointment at two this afternoon with Granny's solicitor, fancy a cuppa before I go?' 'Time for a little cuddle first?' said Max, putting his arms around her again. 'Sorry, I've got to sort out the paperwork, plenty of time when I get back,' Erin replied.
Max sank back down on the sofa and sipped his tea. 'I'm meeting with the dig this afternoon, followed by dinner at the Gatekeeper. I'll see you for breakfast in the morning. Full English breakfast on me at the Coffee Cabin at nine o'clock sharp.'
Erin always enjoyed going to the Coffee Cabin, for a smoked salmon and scrambled egg bagel. The Cabin, a cute little place, was run by a lovely couple and nothing was ever too much trouble. Very popular in the village with the locals, so it was always wise to book a table.

Max sat in his land rover and punched in Cherry's number on his phone. She was not really his type, a bit too prim and proper for his liking, but he was sure he could work his charm on her.
'Hi Max Judd, just wondered if I could come over, I

have a few items we discovered this week which may be valuable, and I thought you could help authenticate them.'

Cherry couldn't help but remember those big blue come to bed eyes and felt a little flattered that he should value her opinion.

'Come by in the morning,' she replied. 'I have a free space between lectures. About eleven?'

'Any chance I could come now? I have to go to Reading in the morning. Maybe we could have dinner after if you're not busy?'

The thought of dinner with the handsome Max Judd swayed her and they agreed to meet at the University at five, when her classes for the day were finished.

He was going behind Erin's back. He knew she would be upset but he had to have the brooch. It was all he thought about, he had to have it no matter what. In the end he was doing it for them, wasn't he?

Erin sat in the Coach and Horses sipping her usual glass of Merlot. She'd managed to get everything tied up with Mr. Barnes, her solicitor and Lavender Cottage had been signed over to her. As she sat there thinking through the day's events a familiar voice came from behind the bar. 'Hello Erin, long time no see.'

'Charlie!' Erin said in surprise, 'What are you doing here?'

Charlie and Erin had been good friends when they were teenagers, He had been her childhood sweetheart at one time, they had been inseparable. Everyone had expected to hear wedding bells, but life took over and they drifted apart. Erin to her nursing and Charlie to his work in marine biology. It must have been at least five years since she had seen him last. The skinny happy go lucky youth of their teenage years had grown into a rather handsome man. He wore his dark hair long in a ponytail and looked very toned. He obviously went to the gym, she thought. Charlie explained that he was between jobs at present and had come back home to Lyminge to see his family. Helping behind the bar was a bonus and a few extra pounds in his pocket. Jo had always liked Charlie, they'd worked together before Charlie left for the Caribbean and he welcomed him back like a long-lost son. It was just like old times.

'You heard about Bill? He's gone missing,' said Mick as Jo drew him a pint. Mick was one of the locals, who lived in the High Street with his wife Norma. If you wanted to know anything you just asked Mick, he was the fount of all local news, being churchwarden.

'Gone missing?' replied Jo, nearly tipping the pint all over Mick.

'Yes, they found his camper on the road to Dover last night. He must have been on his way home from France. He goes there regularly as you know,' Mick said, giving Jo a knowing wink.

Jo felt a little uncomfortable; perhaps his little secret was not so secret after all.

'The camper had been completely stripped and all Bill's belongings were strewed over the road. No sign of Bill, poor old soul, who knows what they have done to him. Police think it was some of those flipping illegal immigrants as many of them have taken to smuggling to earn money. It's possible, but why leave the camper?' continued Mick. 'It's all a mystery.'

Jo couldn't concentrate for the rest of the evening.

Where was Bill? Had he been arrested by the police or even worse killed by the smugglers, he had to find out.

Erin spent an enjoyable evening catching up on all the news. She even treated herself and Charlie to fish and chips whilst he was on his break. Feeling rather full and very rosy, Erin went back to Lavender Cottage where she fell into bed and after lighting her night light fell asleep immediately.

Next morning, she was up bright and early. She washed her hair and put on her new skinny jeans. She felt she needed to make it up to Max for being a bit offhand the previous afternoon. For the life of her she didn't know what had brought it on. Anyway, she felt more like her normal self again today.

Erin got to the Coffee Cabin in plenty of time and sat in the seat she always liked by the window. She ordered herself a latte. Nine o'clock came and went. There was no sign of Max. She called his mobile, but it went straight to voicemail. After three more lattes and a large plate of eggs and bacon, she decided to go home. No doubt he had a good reason, but she couldn't understand why he hadn't called her.

CHAPTER 16

'The victory will soon be yours, do not delay. You must claim her as your own and win the favour of the brooch.'

Max was becoming obsessed with the brooch. He went to bed dreaming about it and woke up thinking about it. It called to him, seemed to take over his emotions and made him do things, anything, even kill, to get his hands on it. He had to have it, whatever the cost. If he couldn't get his hands on the brooch through Erin, he would just have to work on Cherry. She was easy enough to seduce, flattery got him everywhere. Derek had messed up his original plan by getting his hands on the brooch first, but he'd managed to orchestrate his untimely end, by tampering with the brakes on his bike. Telling the story of ash in his helmet was just brilliant. He didn't know whether he believed the stories of the Saxon ghost, but he used it for his benefit with Derek. Strange things certainly seemed to happen around the brooch, but once he'd got his hands on it and made his fortune he wouldn't care. A few more evenings with little Miss Cherry Ripe and he would have her in the palm of his hand. In the meantime, he would tell Erin he'd had to go to the University in Reading to discuss the findings of the dig. That should keep her happy for a while. He liked

Erin a lot, she was one of the best things that had ever happened to him, but that brooch seemed to do something to him. It was as though a red mist came across his eyes and he became a different person. He could see it now, the fame and the fortune when he was awarded the 'Grahame Clark Medal,' by the British Academy for finding the brooch of the Saxon Queen Ethelburga. His name would be known around the world, he would be invited to work with some of the best archaeologists on the most important sites. He must have the garnet brooch, he could think of nothing else.

He had arranged to meet Cherry for lunch in the University Canteen. Not very romantic but needs must. He hoped that this would be the day that he persuaded her to give him the brooch. Sitting sipping a coffee as he waited, he looked round at all the students. 'They just don't know who is sitting in their presence,' he smiled to himself. But one day my name will be known throughout the world as the greatest archaeologist.'

Max and Cherry chatted away like young lovers as they ate their lunch. Max was using all his best lines and Cherry was falling for them. She was butter in his hands. Taking advantage of the moment, Max went in for the kill.

'Any luck with getting approval to have the garnet brooch on loan for our exhibition?' he asked casually.

'I'm still waiting to hear from head office, but I am sure it will be ok', Cherry replied.

'I could really do with it today, if you could possibly do anything. Our exhibition starts tomorrow. It will hold pride of place,' Max said, putting his hands over hers.

The Garnet Brooch

'Well I guess it wouldn't do any harm, it's not as though the University doesn't know you, is it?' said Cherry, as his hands gently stroked hers giving her a warm fuzzy feeling.

An hour later, Max was sitting in his car. 'Well that had been easy,' he thought to himself, a little bit of persuasion and the promise of dinner, the brooch was his. He stared at it wondering what story it would tell. The story of the Hogden family? No. It was his now and it would tell the story of the Judd family.

Max's plan had been to go back to his flat and grab a few things before making his way to his brother's in Bath. He would lie low there until all the fuss had died down and then make his claim. Claim the brooch as his find. Hopefully the professor wouldn't come out of his coma and Miss Cherry Ripe would be too embarrassed by her own stupidity to say anything. A good plan, or so he thought. However, as he sat in the car something kept nagging at him. Nagging him to go to Lyminge, to Erin. So much so the car seemed to suddenly have a mind of its own. No matter how he tried it wouldn't let him drive anywhere but Lyminge. He had no alternative than to be guided down Stone Street. As he looked in the rear-view mirror, he saw the reflection of someone sitting behind him. In his surprise he swerved, nearly missing a tractor coming in the other direction. His hands were shaking, and he felt cold and clammy, so he pulled over on to the grass verge. He turned around nervously, to see who was behind him. There was nobody there; just a small pile of ash on the seat. Looking in the mirror again the reflection was still there but now he realised it was a reflection of himself - himself as a Saxon warrior, with wild hair and a long brown beard. He looked angry and ready to kill.

I'm out of here,' he said, trying to get out of the car, but all the doors were locked and the windows. The only thing he could do was carry on to Lyminge.

CHAPTER 17

Erin received a message from Max saying he had to go to Reading and she decided to use the time to follow up on her Great Uncle George. Mr. Barnes had found an address for him in Granny's papers, so she decided to take a trip to Faversham the next day. Charlie had some free time and said he would love to go with her. She was looking forward to spending more time with Charlie, they had been good friends at school, and it seemed they still had much in common.

Bright and early next morning Charlie stood on the doorstep with a big smile and a large picnic hamper that Jo and Hetty had filled for him the previous night.

'Thought we might find somewhere for a picnic if the rain holds off. Shall I put it in the car?'

'What a lovely idea,' said Erin, grabbing her jacket and car keys. 'I love a picnic.'

Driving down the A2, listening to the sounds of the nineties, they felt like a couple of teenagers again. It didn't take them long to get to Faversham and find Uncle George's bungalow. They hadn't got a phone number so they hoped they would find someone home. Uncle George's bungalow was down by the river, the front garden was well looked after and neatly

The Garnet Brooch

manicured and full of daffodils and tulips. Walking up the path they could see a black and white cat sitting in the window washing his paws. Erin knocked tentatively on the front door with the brass horse head knocker and after a few moments it was opened by an elderly woman in a carer's uniform.

'I'm looking for Mr. George Hogden. He's my great uncle? Is he home?' Erin enquired.

'Oh yes dear, he's just having his morning coffee. Who shall I say is calling?'

'My name is Erin Hogden. Hilda Hogden's granddaughter and this is my friend Charlie.'

'Do come and wait inside, I'll tell him you are here.'

Ten minutes later they were seated round the fire in a very cosy lounge. It reminded Erin of Lavender Cottage when Granny had lived there. Great Uncle George wore a blue and black paisley smoking jacket and looked every part the gentleman. He was so pleased to receive visitors and Erin could tell by the way he spoke that although he was in his late nineties, he still had all his marbles.

'So, you're little Erin. Hilda spoke about you all the time, you were her and Alf's pride and joy. I was sorry not to make her funeral, but my health wouldn't allow it. Blooming arthritis. It's so good to meet you, after all, you are next in the Hogden line. Our sister Joan married of course and had Jonathan, your cousin, but he isn't a Hogden. You're now the keeper of the history of the Hogdens.'

'I'm sad to say that I don't know the family history, Granny and I never got around to talking about it. I guess I was just too busy. How far can you trace the family back?' Erin asked.

'It goes right back to Saxon times, around AD 600 in the reign of Queen Ethelburga.
Our story starts in 633. It's been handed down through the generations. Passed from father to son.'
Great Uncle George sat back in his chair and started telling the story of Elfin and Alfric. A story of love and loss, that centred round the garnet brooch. As he reached the end of the story, he repeated the words of Alfric.
'The garnet brooch will remain as a symbol of our love, I will keep it forever close to my heart and when I die it will be passed from generation to generation. It is always to stay within the Huckbone family. Should the brooch fall into false hands a curse will fall on those concerned, until it is returned. Be warned, I do not give this curse lightly, death and destruction will follow in its wake.'
'Huckbone?' said Erin. 'Our family are Hogdens.'
'There have been many variations of the spelling of Hogden over the centuries. Mediaeval scribes and church officials recorded the name as it sounded. Hockbin, Hogben, Pigbin, Pigpen, Hockburn to name a few. Huckbone was a name given to pig farmers in Saxon times, hence Alfric Huckbone. Today it is spelt Hogden, but not many of us are pig farmers today. We were also great landowners over the centuries, a legacy to be proud of.'

'Granny treasured the garnet brooch and left it to me after she died. Is there anything that can prove it belongs to our family?' asked Erin.
As she looked up, she saw that her great uncle's eyes had begun to get that glazed look. They gradually closed and his chin dropped to his chest as he fell

asleep.

His carer came and took the coffee cups away and placed a warm blanket over his knees. 'That will be all for this morning I am afraid,' she said. 'Perhaps you'd like to call back another day.'

Erin took Great Uncle George's phone number then, leaving hers on the hall table she and Charlie said their goodbyes.

Charlie and Erin decided to drive down to the river to have their picnic as it was such a beautiful afternoon. Hetty had packed the hamper full of all sorts of goodies including a bottle of prosecco. Feeling replete, they lay back on the grass and stared up at the cloudless blue sky as they chatted over all they had heard that morning.

'I now know the story of the garnet brooch,' said Erin, 'but it doesn't help me find the proof of ownership I need.'

'I am sure Great Uncle George will have something,' said Charlie. 'In the meantime, I can do some research online; it's a fascinating story. I'd love to find out what became of Bryce , the baddy in the story too.'

They lay in silence enjoying the spring sunshine for quite a while. Charlie glanced over at Erin, she looked so beautiful lying there beside him, eyes closed, at peace with the world. It was as though she felt his eyes upon her, and she looked at him under her lashes. Charlie reached over and stroked her cheek, 'You're beautiful,' he said as he bent down and kissed her softly on the lips. Erin looked into his eyes and pulled him closer, 'You're not bad yourself,' she smiled as he kissed her again.

The Garnet Brooch

CHAPTER 18

After their picnic Erin and Charlie went back to Lavender Cottage. They were quiet on the way home after their kisses under the sun, but it was a warm, friendly silence as they both thought about their afternoon together. Erin was the first to speak. 'Thank you for a lovely afternoon, I really enjoyed it. About the kisses...'
'I know,' said Charlie reading her mind. 'Let's take it slow. No pressure, no promises just wait and see what happens.'
'Yes, let's wait and see what happens,' Erin replied.

Charlie's shift at the pub was starting at six so he kissed her on the cheek and said he would call her in the morning. He was so happy seeing Erin again. It had broken his heart when she had gone to London to train as a nurse. He had planned to ask her to marry him, but that was not to be. Throwing himself into his work as a marine biologist he had tried to forget her, but she still held a grip on his heart. He found that he still had feelings for her. He hoped she still felt something about him. When he thought of Max Judd, it made him feel angry thinking of them together. It was more than he could bear. As he walked into the bar, Jo was pacing up and down looking very agitated.

'There you are, at last. You're not here just for fun you know, I'm paying you to do a job and I expect you to arrive on time.'

Charlie was taken aback, this wasn't the Jo he knew, what had got him all fired up?

'Sorry Jo. I thought we agreed on six o'clock. Everything ok, you seem a bit tense?'

'Everything's just fine, why shouldn't it be? Go and get a new barrel of 'Spitfire' up from the cellar and then get back here and do your job.'

With that, Jo stormed upstairs. Charlie was right, he was tense, very tense. He'd been round to Bill's again; the camper wasn't anywhere to be seen but Bill and Pat had been in. Pat ushered him into the lounge, where a very drawn and worried Bill sat drinking a cup of tea.

'I'm so sorry Jo, sorry to let you down. I couldn't call you, I lost my mobile in all the kerfuffle and I was absolutely exhausted after walking back from Capel. Only just coming to. I had a really good sleep last night and am feeling a bit more myself today.'

'Tea Jo?' asked Pat, 'still some in the pot. I'll go and pour you one.'

'What the hell happened Bill? I've been worried sick.'

'Pat doesn't know anything, she just thinks the van broke down and I walked home, as I'd lost my mobile and it was late at night.'

Pat returned with Jo's tea. 'I'll leave you two boys to it and go and get some milk from the shop. Won't be long,' she said as she grabbed her purse from the table.

'Ok spill the beans,' said Jo.

'It was around eleven o'clock. I'd just got off the ferry at Dover and was on my way down to you when a blue

The Garnet Brooch

van cut me up and pulled across the road, so I had to stop. Four men in black hoodies pulled me out of the van and pushed me onto the verge. They spoke with an accent, sounded a bit like Polish to me, but it could have been Albanian or Turkish, I'm not sure. I didn't know what to do, I could hardly call the police could I, we'd have both been for it. As I pulled out my mobile to call you, one of the men grabbed it and smashed it under his foot shouting at me to get the hell out of there, or they would break every bone in my body. I started running, running as fast as I could to get some distance between me and the gang. I hid myself behind some trees and watched what was going on. The gang loaded all the stuff into their van, pulling the insides of the van apart, making sure they had everything. Then I heard a police car, someone must have given them a tip off. The gang fled off in their van, but I didn't know what to do. I was worried they could have had me up for smuggling, or even worse found out about our little business, so I stayed hidden.'

'Christ, Bill, what are we going to do now? Have the police been in touch?'

'No, the van is still in Dover and I haven't heard a thing, but I guess it's only time. We can only wait and see what happens, I guess.'

At that point Pat returned with the milk. 'More tea anyone?'

'I was just leaving actually,' said Jo. 'Pop up to the Coach, Bill, when you've got a minute. Thanks for the tea Pat. See you soon.'

He'd been worrying about it ever since, what if they found the goods and the gang, put two and two together and realised Bill was bringing goods into the

country illegally? Their lives would not be the same. He could lose his job, his home and his wife too.
'Oh hell,' he said, as he sat on the sofa, head in hands.

Arriving back at the cottage Erin gave it the once over, all was well or so she thought, until she went upstairs and there, written on the wall in ash, was a message. The message she had seen before.

'Find the truth and set me free, my story will reveal the key. Hold the brooch within your heart, never let it from you depart. It is rightfully yours and not for the taking, after the setting of the sun a new dawn is breaking.'

As she sat down on the bed, she felt a chill in the room, was someone there? The ghost of the Saxon girl? 'I feel you,' Erin said, 'I know your story and I will get the brooch back, but I need your help. I need evidence for the University that it belongs to the Hogden family. Help me please.' As fast as it came, the chill disappeared, and all went back to normal. The message disappeared and Erin was alone. Just then her phone rang, it was Great Uncle George. He had some good news for her. When his mother Eve Hogden had died she had left a letter for him and Alf telling them the story of the garnet brooch. It was written in 1929 so it should prove that the brooch had not just been found but belonged to the family. She had her proof. 'Thank you, thank you,' she said.
Feeling elated, Erin decided to call Max and tell him the good news. She rang and rang, but no answer. She decided to go over to the pub and see Charlie and Jo. She had to tell someone her good news. Charlie was

thrilled and opened a bottle of champagne that Jo kept especially for times like these.

'Where's Jo?' asked Erin.

'Not sure,' said Charlie. 'He's in a very strange mood, I hope he's ok.'

'What are you going to do now?'

'I'll try Max again in the morning, he's probably working and then I'll go and get the letter from Great Uncle George. Hopefully Max and I can go and collect the brooch from the University. 'Good luck', said Charlie, silently wishing that Max Judd would fall off a cliff or something equally disastrous. 'Keep me posted.'

Later that evening Bill came into the bar asking for Jo.

'Haven't seen him, Bill. He may be upstairs, I'll go give him a shout,' said Charlie.

A few minutes later a very bleary-eyed Jo came into the bar, followed by Hetty.

'Jo, thought I'd come straightaway and tell you the news,' Bill said hesitantly, glancing quickly at Hetty.

'It's okay, she knows, Hetty found me head in hands on the sofa and I told her everything. I hope she's going to forgive me.' Jo looked at her hopefully.

'You and me both,' answered Bill, 'Pat gave me a grilling after you left and wanted to know the truth. The long and the short of it is that Pat said it would be best to call the police and tell them I had been set upon on the way back from France, which of course was true. Tell them I had walked home overnight, fleeing from the gang and their threats, hence the delay in reporting the incident. The police took all the details and said after they had been through the van and made their report I could go and collect it.

They asked whether there was anything valuable in the van or anything I'd like to report.

I told them I had some duty-free goods from France and a few electrical items that I had bought Pat as a surprise. A new laptop and fancy hair styler that she had wanted. Their opinion was that this gang were illegals. A lot of the illegal immigrants have taken to doing a bit of highway robbery of late; it was the third this week. They said it was highly unlikely that they would find them as they very quickly went to ground and disappeared from the area, probably going up north. As they know the police are on their trail, they won't hang around long. They hoped my insurance would cover it.'

Jo felt a great weight lift from his shoulders as Bill told him the news. 'Looks like our secret is safe,' he said, breathing a sigh of relief.

'Your secret?' said Charlie, laughing. 'The whole village knows what you two have been doing, have done for months.'

'Well we won't be doing it anymore, will we?' said Hetty, giving Jo and Bill a withering look.

'No, I think we've learnt our lesson, eh Bill?' replied Jo.

CHAPTER 19

'Revenge will be sweet, do not fear. Love will not die; the truth will be ours.'

In the morning Erin called Max again but it kept going to voicemail. By eleven o'clock she decided she could wait no longer, so having left him a message, she went off to collect the letter from Great Uncle George. He was thrilled to see her again. As Mary bought the coffee and cake, he pulled out his old photo albums. 'You've got to look at these,' he said. Two hours later, full of Mary's cake, Erin was on her way to Canterbury. She had rung Max again, but still no answer, so she decided to go to the University on her own. When she arrived, she headed for the Arts and Humanities Department and asked where she could find Cherry Smithers.

Cherry was in the lecture hall, finishing a class on Roman literature, so Erin found a seat and waited outside.

It wasn't long before Cherry appeared under a bundle of papers. 'Excuse me,' said Erin, 'I don't know whether you remember me, I'm Erin Hogden. I came last week with Max Judd to enquire about the garnet brooch.'

'Don't talk to me about Max,' said Cherry, angrily.

'He's gone and left me in one hell of a lot of trouble, as well as taking me for a fool.'

'I don't understand, has he been here then?' asked Erin.

Cherry ushered her through into her office. 'Sounds as though he's taken you for a ride too, goodness knows where he is now. Come on in and I'll tell you what's happened.'

Erin couldn't believe Cherry was talking about the Max she knew and loved. So he had been after the brooch all along. She thought it had all been too good to be true. He had completely fooled her. How could she have been so stupid? Now he had the brooch but where was he?

Back in her car Erin could hold back her tears no longer. Mainly tears of anger at the man she thought loved and cared about her. 'I hate you, I hate you,' she shouted, banging her fists on the steering wheel. She didn't know how long she had sat there but the home time traffic was building up so she guessed it must be about five. Brushing her tears away she started the engine and began her journey home to Lyminge. She was no nearer to getting Granny's brooch back and now she had lost Max too.

The cottage seemed empty and cold so she went over to the pub in the hope a few drinks would drown her sorrows. Propped up at the bar she sat staring at a very large glass of Merlot, and the tears began again. 'It can't be that bad, you'll water down your wine if you're not careful,' said Charlie as he came from behind the bar and put his arm around her. 'Oh Charlie, I've been such a fool, such a fool. What am I going to do?' She buried her face in his T-shirt and cried even harder. It was early and the bar was empty, so Erin was able to tell Charlie and Jo the whole story. Jo was surprised. Max had seemed a good honest guy.

'I've been doing a bit of research on our friend Max Judd.' Charlie cleared his throat. 'Over the last few years he has worked on several digs across the world where valuable artefacts have gone missing. Once challenged he has disappeared, never to be seen again. He has assumed several different names obviously to cover his tracks, one of these names was Borwood. Quite an unusual name so I looked back on the ancestry websites. I was able to follow the line back down the ages through the male line to Saxon times around 655. Although the information was sketchy, there was a Borwood in the archives at Lyminge Church, which held old manuscripts taken from the monastery in the 7th century AD. Now, this is where it gets interesting. Borwood was the Father of Bryce who, if Great Uncle George's story is to be believed, was the man who killed Elfin in the duel with Alfric.'

'Whoa, so you're saying, Max Judd could be a long-lost relative of Bryce? That's unbelievable but it certainly would explain his obsession with the garnet brooch,' replied Erin. 'Still, I must get the brooch back. It belongs in the Hogden family.'

At Charlie's suggestion, Erin rang the police to let them know that Max Judd had stolen the brooch from the university. The university however had already reported the theft. The police confirmed that they were already on the lookout for him, for the murder of

Derek Trott. Evidence had been found showing Derek's motorbike had been tampered with. Max was the prime suspect. They had been to his flat in Canterbury. As yet, there was no sign of him. Erin took a deep breath. She had had a narrow escape – a very narrow one indeed.

CHAPTER 20

'He saw her often in his dreams, the woman that was to be his wife. He saw her in her lover's arms, he saw the brooch binding them together in love. He would have his revenge, separate them for eternity and take the brooch as his own. It was his, Elfin was his.'

Max parked the land rover in the Church car park. It was getting dark as he walked down to Lavender Cottage. Looking in the windows of the Coach he saw Erin and a tall long-haired man. He had his arm around her shoulders, and she seemed to be crying. The man looked at her lovingly and dried her tears on his T-shirt. It made a very touching scene. A surge of white anger went through him and he was amazed how strongly he felt seeing them together. Why was she with him, wasn't she his girl? His own beautiful Erin. He turned abruptly and walked back to the car park. Did they think he couldn't see them?

It didn't matter. After all, when it came to rage and jealousy, Max had a perfect master.

He spent the next few nights in the church, fighting the demons within him. He felt as if there were two people inside him fighting to take control. His head throbbed so much that he thought his brain would burst. Pain and anguish swirled around in his mind, a tide of blood washed back and forth behind his eyes and then the voice, "The garnet brooch, the garnet brooch it belongs to me', over and over. One half of him wanted to run to Erin and apologise and give her back her brooch, whilst the other half of him was turning into a man possessed. A man seeking revenge for the past who will do anything to get what he wanted. He had to see Erin, she had the answers he sought. He had to see her, had to have her, it had been promised, she belonged to him.

After a very restless night, Erin sat curled up on the sofa in her pyjamas. She couldn't believe Max could be capable of murder. He had seemed so genuine. How could she have been taken in like that. Looking down at her phone there was a message from him. 'Hi baby, business all tied up in Reading, so I'm all yours. Be back about ten tomorrow, let's meet at the Coffee Cabin for that breakfast I owe you. Xx'
She looked at the clock. It was a quarter past ten. 'Oh hell, what am I going to do?' She didn't have long to think as there was a loud bang on the door.
'It's me, Max.'
Erin sat glued to her seat, she didn't want to face him knowing everything he had done. What did he want from her, he had the brooch? Was he dangerous? He had killed poor Derek. She'd never liked Derek, but to be killed in that way was awful. The banging grew louder. 'Erin, it's me, come on, open the door.'
She quickly texted Charlie, 'Max at the door. Call me in half an hour, if I don't answer, call the police. Erin.' Keeping all fingers crossed that he would find the message, she opened the door.

The Garnet Brooch

'Morning gorgeous, what happened, overslept?' Max asked, looking down at her pyjamas. 'I'll wait whilst you get dressed and then we can go for a late breakfast.'

'I'm not going anywhere with you, I think we need to talk,' replied Erin. 'I'll make some coffee.'

'What's up, haven't you missed me?' Max asked, reaching for a kiss.

'Missed you? I wish I'd never met you.' Erin answered, turning away.

Max began to look a bit bewildered, what had happened since he'd been away, where was the warm loving woman he had left behind?

'There's no use looking at me with those big blue eyes as though butter wouldn't melt in your mouth, I know what you've been up to and I don't like it. I don't like it at all.

'You are a thief and a murderer. Not only have you taken the brooch from Cherry under false pretences, you killed Derek. How could you?' Erin spat at him.

'Oh, come on, I did it for us baby, I've got the brooch and we can use it to make our fortunes. Just think, we'll be famous.'

'I don't want your fame and fortune, just give me my brooch and leave.'

'You'd like that wouldn't you? I can see it all now. You've got it all planned with lover boy from the pub. Don't think I don't know, I saw you the other night cuddling up in the bar. Well you are mine, do you hear, Erin? Mine. He will not have you or the brooch.'

Erin could see Max was getting agitated, he had a dark look in his eyes and kept opening and closing his fists. It was as though something had control of him. He wasn't the Max she knew and loved. An icy coldness was spreading across the room and the horrible smell had returned. Max stared at her. It was back, the pounding in his head the deep, deep rage rising inside him. Pushing back the chair, he staggered across the room towards her.

'I am keeping the brooch and you are coming with me. We are destined to be together, it was agreed before we were born. Our fathers arranged our marriage. I will be your husband and you will be my wife Elfin.'

' Max, you're frightening me, it's me Erin, Erin Hogden. You are Max Judd, come back to me, do you hear?'

'I am Bryce Borson. Do not anger me Elfin, you will be my wife."

Max grabbed Erin by the wrist. 'Come, we will consummate our marriage here and now, then you will be mine'.

'Leave me alone, Max,' Erin screamed. 'You don't know what you're doing.'

Max pushed Erin to the floor pulling at her clothes, like a man possessed. She fought him off with every ounce of strength she could find, but he was too strong for her.

He stood over her, looking down at her naked body, a look of triumph on his face as he slowly began to remove his trousers. 'You are mine Elfin, now and forever. Do you hear me, now and forever?'

As he lowered himself down on top of her he suddenly froze and stared at something or someone in the corner of the room. He began to shake, and his eyes grew wider and wider in fear. Erin took the opportunity to get up and grabbed the throw from the sofa. She couldn't see anything, but she could feel the presence of someone in the room. Was it Elfin or was it Alfric, come seeking revenge? Max got to his knees, arms held high in a position of surrender and he seemed to speak in another voice.

'Forgive me, I never meant to kill Elfin, she just ran on to my sword. I loved her too, but the garnet brooch clouded my judgement, made me crazy with desire. I have carried the pain through generation to generation, release me, take my life and set me free.'

A primaeval cry echoed around the room and Max fell to the floor, his body convulsing as drool dripped from the corner of his mouth. 'Stop this,' shouted Erin. 'Whoever you are, stop this, and let the past rest in peace. It's time to let go, forgive and set yourself free.' In the corner of the room she could see a figure of a man holding a sword. A woman at his side and she remembered the messages written in ash. Erin spoke into the shadows:

'I know the truth and I set you free. I will keep the brooch close to my heart. It is where it belongs and it will remain with the Hogden family, never to depart. Go now rest in peace, your love will never die.'

Warmth returned to the room and the smell vanished leaving all as it should be. Erin looked down at Max. He was lying surrounded by ash, the garnet brooch by his side. His breathing had returned to normal and he seemed to be sleeping peacefully. Erin picked up the garnet brooch and held it against her heart and she could swear she felt it beating back.

The Garnet Brooch

Her mobile rang, drawing her back into the present. It was Charlie. 'What's going on in there Erin? I'm outside and I heard you screaming?'
' I am ok, everything's fine now,' Erin said in a breathless voice. She drew the blanket tightly around her naked body and went to open the door.
Taking one look at Erin, Charlie burst into the room. 'What the hell's been going on, are you alright, he didn't hurt you or anything did he? I'll kill him if he's done anything to my girl.'
'It's alright Charlie, calm down, it's not like you to get so mad.'
He took her in his arms and held her tight as the rage in him began to fade.
'I am sorry Erin, I don't know what came over me, are you sure you're ok?
'I am, now you're here' said Erin, 'nothing a nice cup of tea won't mend.'
'You go and get yourself dressed and I'll put the kettle on.'
Max was still out cold and lying on the floor covered in ash.
'There's been some weird stuff going on here,' Charlie said as Erin came downstairs. She was still very shaky and tried to explain best she could what had happened but even to herself it all sounded a bit far-fetched. Charlie listened very patiently and held her in his arms. 'It's over Erin. I'm here, all will be well. I think we'd better call the police again though.
They've been looking for your Max Judd.'
Max began to wake up. His eyes were still glazed with fear and he seemed unable to speak. Erin tried talking to him, but he just babbled incoherently, pointing at

the corner of the room. Try as they might, they could get no sense out of him. Even when the police arrived, he was still staring into the corner. They thought he must have had a fit or a stroke, so they called an ambulance to take him away. Max didn't say a word, he just sat there looking like a rabbit caught in headlights and as they put him in the ambulance he never even looked back.

CHAPTER 21

2019

All was quiet at the cottage after everyone had left. Erin sat down and stared around. No ghostly figures or funny smells; everything had returned to normal. Charlie sat with her, his arm protectively around her shoulders. 'How are you feeling now lovely, you looked awful when I got here?'
'I'm so glad you're here Charlie, I don't know what I would have done without you, you've been a brick.'
'That's what friends are for,' he replied, drawing her closer.

The police had taken the brooch with them to authenticate ownership. The University had reported it missing and so enquiries needed to be made and her family letters examined before the brooch could be released to her. Professor Crump was now back at work having made a full recovery. The doctors were mystified as to his problem but put it down to a virus that had caused him to collapse and go into a coma. The ash they put down to him having knocked a jar of ashes off the shelf as he fell onto his desk. All very strange.

Max had been taken into custody and charged with

robbery, murder and fraud. However, as he was not in his right mind he was taken to a secure facility for medical care until he was mentally stable to face the charges.

Erin still couldn't believe the Max who had been so loving and kind had turned out to be a killer and a thief. The power of the garnet brooch had possessed him, body and soul. Her heart still ached as she remembered their times together, she thought she had found her Mr. Right. Nothing ever seems to work out as you expect; who could imagine the story of the garnet brooch? A story Erin would keep in her heart and maybe one day write down to pass on to the next generation of Hogdens.

The following day, Erin and Charlie walked hand in hand up to the churchyard. Erin had picked some flowers from the garden to lay on Granny's grave and as they arrived, she noticed primroses had sprung up around the headstone.
'I'm sure they weren't there before,' she said as she bent down to take a closer look. 'I wonder who planted them?'

They sat down on the bench under the chestnut tree. Neither said a word, they just sat and listened to the silence. The wind rustled through the leaves of the tree and seemed to whisper on the breeze. 'Thank you,' it said. 'You found the truth and set us free. Thank you, thank you.'

Charlie bent down and kissed Erin gently on the lips.

'What will you do now, go back to London?' he asked.
'No, I think I'll stay around a while and see what develops,' she replied, giving him a cheeky smile. 'The hospital has put my job on hold for now, which will give me time to plan what I will do next.'
'I hope those plans will include me,' he said as he took her in his arms and kissed her again

Today as you walk through the churchyard and see the primroses maybe you will think of Erin and Charlie and the story of the garnet brooch.

ABOUT THE AUTHOR

Local writer Katherine Goody lives in Kent with her husband Roger and little dog Teddy. Her love of creative writing started after she retired, and she has written many short stories and poems that are printed in several local anthologies.

Katherine has also written a memoir, entitled 'I Met Him at the Well', published in 2018. Which is the story of how her life changed dramatically when she became a Christian, and how God has used her to share his love at home and abroad.

'Peter the Pony' was published in 2021 and is a story for children aged 4-11 years encouraging them that they are loved and special. Katherine has had the privilege of holding book readings at local schools sharing Peter's story.

The Garnet Brooch is her longest fictional piece yet. It tells the tale of two women centuries apart whose lives are linked by a garnet brooch. Elfin a young woman from the Saxon times, ill-fated in love and Erin from the 21st century who is searching for the truth behind the brooch.

Katherine has endeavoured to make the historical facts as true as possible, however The Garnet Brooch is entirely fictional. All names and characters are from her imagination, with the exception of Queen Ethelburga. Places mentioned are true and are included to centre the story entirely in the village of Lyminge and surrounding area

The Garnet Brooch